The Middle of Nowhere

The Middle of Nowhere

SID GARDNER

"Where'd All The Good People Go"; © Jack Johnson Music.
Used With Permission

iUniverse, Inc.
Bloomington

The Middle of Nowhere

iUniverse books may be ordered through booksellers or by contacting:

iUniverse
1663 Liberty Drive
Bloomington, IN 47403
www.iuniverse.com
1-800-Authors (1-800-288-4677)

ISBN: 978-1-4620-4009-4 (pbk)
ISBN: 978-1-4620-4010-0 (ebk)

Printed in the United States of America

iUniverse rev. date: 07/20/2011

Foreword

This book is dedicated to the 14,000 girls who live every day what the book presents as fiction.

In many ways, these are the most fascinating, tragic girls in our nation. They have been abused, neglected, prenatally exposed to drugs or alcohol, or born with mental and emotional burdens few of us have to carry. Some of them are beautiful and brilliant, but what has happened to them has robbed them of the ability to believe that they are either attractive or smart. Some are the children, biological or adopted, of caring people who have dedicated a large part of their lives to giving these girls a chance. And some of them are the children of profoundly selfish semi-adults who should have been prohibited by law from ever pretending to be parents.

Some of these girls have been so brutalized that they suspect everyone they meet intends them harm. Some have acquired survival and manipulative skills that would make them world class spies, guerillas, or thieves. Or outstanding lawyers, actresses, or CEOs of their own companies.

Suddenly going off to live for several months or for years in a distant "home" that is never a home is a shattering experience. For many of these girls, it comes as the latest of a series of betrayals and rejections that tell them over and over that they are not wanted and they cannot be part of a normal family. Their anger is invariably life-long, and easy to understand.

Yet some are also gloriously funny, able to laugh at themselves and their peers, with their humor honed to a sharp point that can sometimes protect them from further harm. For mid- to late-teenagers, they can be stunningly articulate as they tell their many stories about being in a place that one of them called, in a moment of incandescent clarity, "the middle of nowhere."

These are stories from the middle of nowhere. Nowhere: not only living in a place that is far away, but living disconnected, being lost, and alone. And these are also stories about the people that try to help these girls build a bridge back to somewhere better.

"Where'd all the good people go?"
Jack Johnson

Part One

1

March

A car pulled up to the front of the two-storied house. A short, stocky woman and a young girl got out of the car. The woman motioned to the girl and moved toward the front door. Holding a small gray suitcase, the girl stood by the car, looking around at the house and the hills beyond. Her shoulders slumped, and she slowly walked up the concrete path to the house, tugging her jacket around her against the cold, windy afternoon.

The house looked new up against the early spring-green hills a mile away. Beside the house, four horses grazed in a few acres of grass. Three similar houses stood further down the street, spaced evenly around a cul-de-sac, with stables behind the last house. Off in the distance, cattle seemed motionless in a fenced area nearer the hills.

The cluster of buildings was austere, with careful landscaping and curved driveways in front of each house. A small sign at the head of the street concealed more than it revealed, saying simply "The Houses."

A row of small, gabled windows peered out from the second stories. As the girl stepped onto the front porch, she saw a curtain on one of the windows move aside for a moment, and then quickly drop back into place.

To the east, the foothills rose up beyond the houses into a cloudless sky. Further on, but concealed by the foothills, a much higher mountain range marked the edge of the great basin of the Southwest. To the west, the high desert flattened out to the horizon, with a few rocky buttes the only interruption in the monotonous flow of land. Cactus and sagebrush prevailed, making the wooded mountains to the east seem more inviting once they came into view.

But the mountains could not be seen from the houses, and they were far from the daily routines of the girls who lived there. Two or three times in the winter, the girls piled into a van and went off to play in the snow. For the rest of the year, however, the mountains were part of the further world from which the girls had been removed. They longed for the mountains nearly as much as they longed for what passed for home. But they had to be satisfied with the hills behind the houses. And in front of them, when they looked out the windows, the vast spaces of the high desert reminded them how far the houses were from home.

Each house had a name, and the first one on the street, where the car had stopped, was "Prospect." As the girl and the woman entered the wide hallway at the front of the house, they saw a large, formal room off to the right. At the end of the hallway, stairs rose to the second floor. With the woman leading the way, they moved down the hallway into the house. Small offices were lined up to the right, and then on the left, the space opened into a large kitchen and family room. Over a fireplace, a TV was mounted on the wall. Behind the kitchen were the live-in family quarters, a one-bedroom apartment separated from the rest of the house by a door with a combination keypad. The house was silent, without any sound other than soft talking behind one of the office doors.

Ten girls lived in the house with a married couple. Four additional staff came in during the day to supervise the girls as they did their chores, attended school, and participated in therapy sessions.

They called the house a home—a "residential home."

2

Lexie

When I got there, I looked around and thought to myself, there's not going to be any running away from this place—I'd just run into a bunch of freaking cows.

The woman they hired to take me on the plane was nice enough, I guess. She did this for a living, so she'd been to the place before. After we landed and drove west from the airport for an hour or so, she pulled up to this house with a sign on the front door that said Prospect. A big house, just like three other houses next to it, out in this open place with some horses and a lot of dirty brown hills behind it.

I was sad, pissed at my parents, and worried about what was going to happen next. I still didn't believe I was really there. Five hours ago I was at home, an hour ago I was on an airplane taking me to a place where I was pretty much stuck for the next year or so, if I could believe what my parents and the counselor at the hospital had told me. A year!

I wouldn't miss my school much, for sure, but I would miss a few of my friends a lot. And maybe I would miss my parents sometimes and even my rotten sister, who was older, and prettier, and about fifty degrees meaner than me.

I carried my suitcases in, and then the husband and wife who lived in the house and ran the place came into the front room—they told me later that they called it "the fancy room"—and introduced themselves. The escort lady signed some papers and then left.

The house parents were named Sue and Sam, and in all the time I spent there, I never figured them out. Their names were stupid, first of all—who marries someone who makes your names sound like a cleaning product? They were mostly nice, on the surface, but when they got mad, the nice turned mean very fast. I learned to watch out for the change.

3

Annie

Annie Salinas walked slowly through the front door, greeted by a louder version of the faint shrieking she had heard as soon as she stepped out of her car in the staff parking lot. She had little desire to rush into whatever crisis had boiled over. She knew the morning staff was either handling the explosion well—or had screwed it up so badly that it would take hours for the girls to settle down.

Annie had worked at The Houses for five years, making her senior to all the rest of the House staff. She had received three pay raises, and a year ago she had been promoted to running a therapy group for girls who lived in Prospect.

After graduating from the social work program at Cal State Fullerton in Orange County, Annie took the first job that came along that guaranteed that she could work directly with girls. She was the youngest of four children in a family from Santa Ana. Annie had worked at a shelter for runaway girls in the evenings all through college. She loved the work, and had thought that working at The Houses would bring the same rewards.

Annie knew she was good at what she did. She brought a no-nonsense attitude to the job of dealing with strong-willed, emotionally scarred girls, while being able to coax nearly all of them into confiding in her when they hit bottom.

She was about 5'4" tall, with long dark hair that she usually wore in a braid. She had heard one of the girls call her "Pocahontas" when she thought Annie couldn't hear her. Proud of her Indian blood from her

Mexican ancestors, Annie was secretly pleased with the label—especially after she heard the nicknames for some of the rest of the house staff. She dressed in bright colors, both to cheer up the depressing atmosphere of The Houses and because she loved the colors of her family's native Vera Cruz.

Annie's grandfather had come up to work in the fields of the Central Valley in California during the 1940's, as part of the wartime *bracero* program. He had taken advantage of the 1965 immigration law changes to bring the rest of his family up from Mexico, and became a citizen as soon as he could. Annie and her grandfather had become very close before he died, and they had long talks about the balancing act facing every Mexican family living in California.

"Anna Maria," he once said to her in words she never forgot, "you are going to be one of the ones who can be *una salvadora*, a rescuer, to help the rest of us in this strange land. You will be a guide to show us how all our children can have a better life. And you must help those who have lost the way to find the right path."

But now, as she walked into the front hallway in Prospect House, she wasn't so sure she wanted to rescue any of the lost ones—either the girls or the staff. Sometimes she thought some of the staff needed at least as much help as the girls. More than once she had pulled a staff member aside to suggest a different way of handling a girl who had lost control. Annie had an instinctive way of defusing an angry girl, knowing that soft answers indeed turned away wrath, and that some of the girls felt most alive when they were confronting someone in authority. The other staff members often got sucked into spiraling, escalating conflicts, which only made things worse. Whenever she could, Annie tried to show them how to disengage from a verbal battle, saving face and yet able to back away.

For Annie knew more than she wanted to about these girls, because she had lost her own sister to the streets.

4

Lexie

That first night was hell. Sue, the house parent, took me upstairs and showed me where to put my stuff. I had half of a little room with a small closet, a chest of drawers, a bed and a window. When I pulled the curtain aside, all I could see out of the window was the little hills behind the house and a few other houses. My family used to go on dumb camping trips up in the Sierra, so I was used to big mountains. But these were just little hills like they have in Southern California where we live.

My area was separated from the rest of the room by a half-wall between me and my roommate, Amanda somebody. There were little plastic things on the walls with blinking lights. Sue pointed to them and said "Those are the motion detectors."

So now they didn't even want us to move.

I went back downstairs with Sue into a big room off the kitchen. They called it the family room, but there was no family there—there was just a bunch of girls. Most of them had on t-shirts or baggy sweatshirts that said The Houses in small print.

Sue introduced each of them, but I was too nervous to catch most of their names. There were two very tough-looking girls about six feet tall, some about my size—5 feet 3 inches—and some who looked foreign. I later found out that there were girls there and in the other houses that had come from Russia, Mexico, India, and other countries. About a third of them were adopted.

We had a snack, some kind of chewy granola bar that tasted like paste, and then someone turned on television. We watched a boring program on whales, while one of the girls quietly explained to me that we were only allowed to watch nature shows and quiz programs. The girl, who said her name was Laurie, was from Riverside. She was short, and kind of cute. She had a squeaky little voice that was annoying until you got used to it.

Then dinner was served—the first of too many forgettable meals, I would learn. Hot dogs, string beans, watery milk, and peel-top pudding cups.

It was a TV night, so we watched more TV. Prairie dogs, this time, not whales. The other girls talked softly to each other, but no one talked to me. After the program was over, one of the night staff whose name was Evelyn, said "Everyone in rooms, lights out at 8:30."

8:30! What the hell was that about—at 8:30 back home I was just getting started with online chat and looking for new music. What was I going to do all night?

As the girls were picking up their stuff and starting upstairs, Evelyn turned to me and said "Lexie, come into the office. I need to brief you on the house rules."

Brief me? Like this was some kind of army or something? I kept quiet and walked into this little room around the corner from the kitchen. There was a chart with each of the girls' names on the wall with some numbers after the names. Mine was on the bottom, with no numbers.

Evelyn saw me looking at the chart and said "That's the point system we use here. Everybody gets points for doing what they're supposed to—and loses them when they don't."

"So what is it we're supposed to do?"

Right away it looked like one of the things we weren't supposed to do was ask questions, because she got an irritated look on her face and said, in a very Mom tone, "I was about to explain that."

She droned on, telling me how you get points, and how they can get taken away. It sounded like the homeroom advisor back at my old high school or one of my parents telling me the rules. I zoned out, and she seemed to notice after a while.

"Let's talk about you, Lexie. Why are you here?"

It was such a stupid question. It shouldn't have made me cry. But it almost did, and probably that's what she was trying to do. Later I figured out that they were going to keep asking me this question over and over until I came up with something that they thought was the right answer. But right then, I didn't want to talk about my so-called disorder. So I blurted out, "Because I kept running away from home and ditching school and breaking my parents' stupid rules."

"What kind of rules?"

"I have to stop using the phone at 9:30 and be in bed by 10:30 on school nights. And I have to always let them know where I am. And they made me drink milk at every meal."

It sounded so dumb, I know. And Evelyn knew that, and just let my pathetic answer hang out there without saying anything. Finally she said. "Wow. Milk and no late phone calls. What a rough life."

It was such a bitchy comment I wanted to slap her. I thought she wanted me to open up, but she just put me down. So screw her. "I'm done talking about this."

"Maybe for now, Lexie, but we'll have to come back to it."

"Fine. Later. I'm going to bed now." And I stomped off upstairs.

5

Annie

A new girl had arrived the day before, and Annie was assigned to have an initial one-on-one orientation session with her before the staff psychologist saw her for the first time. When the new girl, named Alexandra Crockett, walked into the staff office on her second day at Prospect, Annie said, "Please sit down, Alexandra. My name is Annie Salinas and I'm the senior house staff in Prospect."

"Lexie—I go by Lexie," the girl said. She was sullen, as Annie fully expected from a girl just beginning her stay at The Houses. As Annie watched her, she saw that Lexie was quite pretty, with dark brown, shoulder-length hair and brown eyes. Her skin was as clear as a two-year-old's.

Annie noticed Lexie looking around the room at Annie's walls. There were some family pictures of Annie with her sisters and parents, a picture of sunset behind the pier at Balboa in Orange County, and a framed medal from a half-marathon. A big whiteboard covered most of one wall. The words on it said "Want control? Get yourself under control."

"Tell me why you're here, Lexie."

"Again?! I had to go through all that crap with Evelyn last night. Don't you people ever talk to each other?"

Annie picked up the anger, which had quickly replaced the sullenness. She mentally added some new entries to Lexie's portfolio. Articulate, enjoys arguing—like most of the girls—and wasn't afraid to mix it up with adults, whoever they were. Annie looked at the file folder in her lap, which had been sent by the psychiatric hospital where Lexie had been treated before she was referred to The Houses. Bipolar, ADHD, artistic, above average intelligence but failing most classes at her high school because she ditched all the time. And an athlete; Lexie had run cross-country and had not been bad at it.

"You run?"

"You talking about track or running away?" Back to sullen, but looking carefully at the half-marathon medal.

"Whichever you want to talk about." Annie decided to get past the sparring and try to make contact. "Lexie, my job is to find out what we can do here to help you get home. We need to develop a treatment plan, and so I'll be working with Dr. Gustafson, the therapist who visits each of the girls once a week. To do that I need to know more about where you're coming from, and find out what you want to work on while you're here."

"I want to work on getting the hell out of here."

"Sensible goal. So how can we help you with that?"

"How long do I have to be here?" Now Lexie's tone shifted from aggressive to pleading.

"It depends on how hard you work. Some people are here a year or longer, some as little as six months. It's mostly up to you and how much progress you make. Not everybody gets better here, Lexie. But the ones who do the work here get the payoff when they get home."

Lexie settled back in her chair, still wary, but visibly calming down in response to Annie's soft approach and her focus on the goal of going home. Lexie began talking about being bipolar and how unfair she thought it was. She used a phrase Annie had read before in the literature on bipolar depression—black dog days. It was borrowed from Winston Churchill, but many bipolars had taken it for their own. From what she had seen in her own family, Annie thought it was a great description.

6

Lexie

I'm supposed to be doing this stupid journal, writing down "my feelings." As if I would ever let any of these creeps read what I really think. One of the girls warned me that when they get mad at you, some of the staff will take your journal and read out loud from it in therapy. They're not supposed to, but no one does anything about it when they do.

So I'm writing what is more or less safe—about my "disorder." BP disorder is what I have, a fancy-sounding bunch of letters for bipolar depression. I call it my black pissing dog days. We had to read this biography of Winston Churchill in one of my history classes, and he called his depression his black dog days. Pretty good description of it. Something big crushes you down, you don't want to get out of bed, and when you do, you feel like you're dragging it around behind you all day long. So you lash out at whoever bugs you—your mom, your dad, your sister—or some so-called friend who's annoying you. When I'm in the middle of black dog times, everything is annoying—the color of the paint on the walls, people's voices, even the sunshine.

I tried hard to keep myself under control, but sometimes I just completely lost it. I get so furious about whatever sets me off—usually my parents saying no to something I want. It jumps from being frustrated that I can't get what I want to hating anyone who says no to me, hating my house, hating everything about my life. I would get so angry that I almost felt like I was blacking out, like my whole body was screaming at a level that no one but me could hear. And when that happens, all that I cared about was getting rid of the anger, the venom that had built up in my body and my brain. And then I would say things to my mom and dad and Justine that were horrible—things I would never dream of saying when I was back to normal. And sometimes even the vicious words weren't enough, and then I just wanted to break things. I would grab something and throw it. I broke three phones throwing them at the wall in our house, and I flushed two of my dad's cellphones down the toilet. It cost hundreds of dollars to fix the stopped-up toilet and hundreds more to replace the phone.

My mom once called it the "raging reds side" of my black dog days.

Just before I went into the hospital, it got so bad I was trashing my room every few days or so, breaking stuff in the house, and kicking holes in the wall. My room looked like a war zone. The cops came to our house three times in one week, and I know our neighbors thought I was a total nut case. And I guess sometimes I was.

My mother told me one day that my grandmother—my dad's mom—was "moody" and had been mean to my dad when he was growing up. She never said it, but I guessed she had meant to imply that it was Grandma's fault that I had inherited the bipolar stuff. But my dad never talked about it.

When I get wound up and pissed off, there are only two things that could calm me down. The first is music. But they have these dumb rules here about when you can listen to music. Usually when I need it most, they won't let me have it. At home, I could go to my room, lie down on my bed, and put on headphones to listen to the music I like—some rap, some hard rock, some softer stuff. But here, you have to earn music privileges, and I haven't earned much yet.

Running sometimes calms me down, too. It's funny—I got sent here partly because I run away and sneak out of the house at night and hang out with friends—a crummy grade of friends, some of them. But when I get mad at my parents or sick of being in our boring house, I can almost always cool down by running on a track or along the edge of the river bed by our house.

My therapist—or I guess the junior therapist, this chick named Annie something—says I can learn to get out from under the black dog days by taking control of my life. That's a weird thing to tell someone in a place where they take away every last bit of control you have over your life. I'm supposed to learn how to control myself and how not to lose control by giving up control to the people who run this place.

None of it makes any sense. You're home, and then they come in the night like you're a criminal and they take you and put you into a car and take you to the airport. You fly with an "escort"—who's really a guard. Then they drop you in some house a thousand miles from home. And you get there and they say now you're in control of your life. Right.

Sometimes I just wish the people who are supposed to be in charge here had to go through one day of living the way we do, under their stupid rules. Just one day.

7

Annie

Once a month Annie was required to go to the central offices of The Houses in Desert City for staff development, which was a fancy word for training. A lot of the curriculum was just a repeat of things she had learned in her social work program in college, so Annie usually tucked some of her stationery in her notebook so she could write letters to her family and friends during the boring lectures.

But this month, a young man from the research staff was giving a presentation. Annie watched him as he set up the LCD projector for the inevitable PowerPoint show in the large conference room in the central office complex.

Annie wondered how people ever taught before PowerPoint came along. She had read somewhere that PowerPoint presentations were what convinced somebody the U.S. should invade Iraq. The point was—pun intended—that PowerPoint presentations make everything seem easy by leaving out a lot, using the bullet points and cute animated pictures and numbers that fly into charts, so that people get persuaded that things are simpler than life really is. The criticism sounded right to Annie.

The staff group filed into a large conference room at the headquarters office. After an introduction by Suzanne Ellison, the program director of The Houses, the young man began his presentation. His name was Greg Wisnewski, and Annie noticed from her seat at the other end of the table that he was tall and reasonably good-looking, though he was starting to lose some of his hair in the front. But he had a good mouth, and Annie thought that if she had learned anything in her quarter century plus, it was that mouths were very, very important.

"Today I want to make sure we all have some context for our work—some real numbers." He touched his laptop and a slide came up: "There are 25 million youths aged 12-17 in the US. In the last year, an estimated 2.6 percent of these youths received out-of-home services for emotional or behavioral problems in a hospital, a residential treatment center, or a foster care setting—a total of 658,000 youth. Of these, about 12 percent spent more than 25 days in a treatment setting, totaling about 78,000 youth."

Wisnewski went on. "About 1 percent of all youth spent time in a residential treatment center—about 250,000 youth, and of these, about 9.5 percent, or 24,000, spent more than 25 days in such a setting. These are the youth who make up the long-term residential treatment population.

"Of the kids who have stayed in one of these kinds of facilities for more than 25 days, 56% are female. Assuming those percentages hold in residential treatment, there are about 14,000 girls in these facilities at any point in time." He paused to let the numbers sink in, then leaned forward. "These are our girls—the girls in our programs."

Annie heard the emphasis he had placed on the word "our." It was an unusual way for a researcher to talk, and she began listening to him more carefully. The number rang in her head. 14,000 girls like the girls in Prospect House. 14,000.

"The residential treatment field is widely diverse, ranging from some of the best programs," he smiled slightly, "among which we would classify ourselves—to some much less professional, unaccredited organizations. One of the best ways to assess these programs is whether they do any follow-up studies on the outcomes of treatment." His voice got an edge. "Whether they care enough to count what happens to the girls who were in their care.

"It's easy to fudge the numbers, and a lot of programs do it. If you start by screening out girls who might not succeed, and if you measure stability as meaning girls went home or moved into an apartment and you can find them six months later—then these programs achieve a two-thirds to 80% success rate. But those are phony numbers."

Suzanne, who was sitting beside Greg at the head of the conference room table, broke in, "Greg, I'm sure you didn't mean to leave the impression that we or any other programs we work with would deliberately publish inaccurate data."

Annie saw a mixture of annoyance and concern on Greg's face. "No, I didn't mean that. But I do want to emphasize that long-term follow-up is the acid test of whether or not a program believes in itself and wants to improve itself by measuring what matters. What matters is whether these girls who enter treatment ever stabilize over the longer term, not just whether they graduate from a program and go home."

He had stood up to Suzanne, and Annie found herself admiring the guy. After glancing at his left hand and noticing no ring, she decided to talk to him after the meeting. Greg took questions for ten minutes longer, and then the meeting ended. Annie stood up and began making her way to the front of the room, tucking a stray strand of hair into her silver clip.

8

Lexie

At first, the other girls were all cliquey, just like high school. But they were weird cliques, and there was some stuff going on that I didn't get at first, two or three girls who would always hang out with each other and always seemed to be touching each other. Later, one of the girls explained the phrase "gay for the stay," which she said meant that some girls had decided they were bisexual and were going to have lesbian hookups while they were in the treatment program. One of the bi's came up to me after I had been there a few days and said "Are you straight or cool?" I had no idea what to say, so I just laughed and walked away. Another one asked me, early in my stay at The Houses, "Can you see the rainbow?" I guess that was code for being gay.

It seemed pretty yucky to me at first, but after a while I got used to that, too. Once you told them you were straight, and never gave the impression that you thought they were perverts or anything, they stopped bothering me about it, and it became sort of normal.

The other cliques were also hard to figure out at first. But then I began to recognize which ones were the girls who had been hard druggies and liked to talk about it a lot. One of the counselors called it "drugalogues." I could tell which ones were into books and academics, which were the artists, and which ones were jocks who lived for the soccer games we had with the normals from local high schools.

I even got pushed into a sort of clique myself, because there was this geographic thing where people got classified based on where they were from. Since I was from Orange County, one of the tougher girls from Oakland one day called me "Laguna Barbie," and it stuck. One of the other girls was from San Clemente, and we knew a few of the same people, so we got to be sort of friends. Her name was Holly, but they called her Laguna Barbie 2. It was better than "stupid white bitch," which was the sweet little phrase that came out of the mouth of one of the wannabe gangbangers from one of the other houses once when I irritated her in class.

The wannabes didn't worry me because I had gotten to be friends with the biggest girl in our house, Belinda Hutchison. One of the druggies from another house came up to me one day in the lunch room after I had been there for a few weeks and said "I heard you were a snitch, and I'm going to kick your ass." Belinda, who was from Kentucky, was about 6'1" and weighed around 220, walked slowly across the room where this was happening and said "I don't think you are, you skanky ho, unless you think you can kick my ass, too." Word got out, and Belinda was my bodyguard from then on. She was into hairdressing and I had let her experiment on me, so we were buds.

But it was more than the cliques. Each girl had her own thing. Belinda was explaining it to me one night while we were sitting in the kitchen talking quietly during a stupid movie neither of us wanted to watch. "You know, some of these girls are really weird," she said.

"Like who?"

She looked at me and then frowned. I could tell she was trying to make up her mind about how much to tell me. She pointed at me, and said "You can't talk about this, you know."

"I know."

"That one?" she pointed to the cute one from Riverside who had spoken to me the first day I got here. "She's the button-pusher."

"What does that mean?"

"Laurie knows just what to say to make the staff go crazy. Wait 'til you see her do it—she makes them so pissed they can't even talk straight. And she looks so innocent when she does it, she never seems like she's being defiant or losing control."

She nodded to another one who was playing with an iPod. They let you have iPods if you get to a certain level. "Sheila is the hacker. I don't know what she does—I just know she can get into any computer anywhere. I've seen her do it."

"On the office computers?" I was amazed, because they had told me when I first arrived that one of the big rules was that no one was allowed to use the office computers, and the classroom computers didn't have any access to the internet unless the teacher was standing right over you and typed in the code.

"No. Maybe she'll explain it to you if she gets to trust you. She did something to the classroom computers and set up some kind of satellite downlink that the staff doesn't know about. She let me use it once or twice to email my boyfriend."

"Wow. That's totally awesome."

She was talking a lot about the others, but I wanted to ask her about what she wasn't saying. "So what's your deal?"

"Me?" She shook her head, her long hair rippling along her metal-covered ear. "I see through people. My dad used to say I have a great BS detector. I see what people mean, no matter what they say."

I nodded, "I used to have a shrink who called that emotional intelligence. It means you can read people better than the rest of us."

"Yeah? Maybe that's it." She looked over at the other girls and then at Kendra, the staff person who was monitoring them. "But it's not always a good thing to know when people are lying to you. Means you end up not trusting anybody very much."

She was frowning and clearly wanted to change the subject. She pointed to another girl who was dark-skinned, from India or Pakistan or somewhere. "Laila is a poet. She leaves haiku everywhere."

"Haiku?" I remembered writing poetry in an English class my freshman year. "You mean poems, 5-7-5 syllables or something like that?"

"Yeah. Wait, she left one in class today. I keep them because some are very funny and she just throws them away." She pulled a scrap of paper out of her jeans, and I read

Stuck here in the sand
Horse shit piled in the corral
Oh how lovely.

I started to laugh and Belinda shushed me. "Don't. She hates it when people comment on her work."

Sometimes the girls talked to each other about where we had been before. Most of the girls had been to local hospitals or other residential programs, and some had been in day treatment programs.

I hated it in the psychiatric hospital where my parents put me after I snuck out and stayed out for four days of serious partying. The hospital was a part of the California University system and was only a few miles from our house in Orange. But it felt like I was on the moon.

There were seven other kids in there when I checked in. They were there for all kinds of different things—cutting themselves, attacking their parents, and drugs. One of them had his arm all bandaged up. He'd been in a knife fight with a friend of his after using meth.

But I guess maybe they thought I was weird, too.

There were two orderlies there all the time during the day—a guy and a woman, both stocky and mean-looking. The doctor came to see us once a day and the psych nurses were always asking us questions about how we felt. The food was OK, but they never served anything that I liked.

They were always taking blood samples to check out lithium level and thyroid level and all kinds of levels. My arms got sore from all the needles—we learned to try to delay the blood work until late afternoon because there was this one nurse who came on duty at 3 who was really good at it. The rest of them just jabbed it in and didn't care if it hurt you.

But there were some kind of funny parts, too.

When my mom and I used to go shopping, we usually went to this big upscale kind of place in Newport Beach with Mercedes and BMWs parked all over the place. And I finally got used to seeing people walking through the shops talking to themselves—once I realized that they were Bluetoothing on their phones.

Then I got to the psychiatric hospital. There, it dawned on me that the people that I saw talking to themselves really were talking to themselves—or to some imaginary friends—and not Bluetoothing.

It was very confusing. After two weeks there, I knew I never wanted to go back there. One of the temp nurses said something when I first got there that sounded like just another slogan when I first heard it, but it kept going around in my head. He said, "Lexie, your behavior got you here and your behavior can get you out." It was a slogan—but some slogans are right.

I talked to some of the other girls in Prospect, Belinda mostly, and sometimes to Amanda, my roomie. We'd all had the same kind of experience in school. Early on—maybe about third grade—there was this change when they started to divide us up into normals and specials. They may have been some of the smartest kids in the school, like Monica and Laurie, but their ADHD or meltdowns or something that was different got them all marked as specials.

And it didn't really mean special—it meant sub-standard. And we knew it. And when they put a label like that on you, you either got into a little shell by yourself or you try to be cool by making jokes or doing outrageous things. And as you get older, the outrageous things creep over the line into sex and drugs. And they catch you, sooner or later, and then the label gets printed in bigger letters, and you're marked, for as long as you're at that school.

Some of the girls had tried what the AA people call "doing a geographic"—trying to move away from the places where they had been labeled as troublemakers or weird. It almost never worked, because the same stuff that had marked you in the old place popped up in the new place, and teachers got your records from the old place, and they treated you like you were special. And then the whole cycle started all over again.

So I wondered what would happen when I got back. Would the label be even bigger this time? Would I be THE WEIRDO WHO GOT LOCKED UP?

9

Annie

Annie was leading a group session after school, and everyone was supposed to talk about their goals. Dolores was from Arizona and had been sent to The Houses because of her problems in school, refusing to attend and attacking teachers and other kids when she got frustrated. When it was her turn, she gave a small laugh and said "I don't have any goals. I guess I'll just drop out of school when I get back and live on the street. No rules, no schedules, no curfew. My ideal."

Annie was furious. She pounded on the table, and a few of the girls actually jumped back. "Don't you ever say that! That's an ignorant thing to say. Some of these girls may not want to talk about it, but they can tell you more than you ever wanted to know about what it means to live on the streets." She paused, weighing whether to go on. "I know a hell of a lot about what it means—I've walked up and down every street in Santa Ana looking for my sister. Don't you ever glamorize living on the streets—it means having running sores and filthy hair and bugs all over your body and peeing in alleys! Sound glamorous?"

Three of the girls who had been there longer had heard Annie go on like this, but the newer ones were amazed at her passion and anger. Dolores glared at Annie and said "Just kidding—chill, dude."

Annie knew she had over-reacted and tried to move the group on by calling on the next girl. But as she did, she tuned out of the girl's response and found herself drifting back to the memories she had tried so hard to escape.

Annie was the youngest of four girls, and Irene was the oldest. Before Annie started school, Irene often baby-sat her while their mother and father both worked. Annie had crystal-clear memories of Irene reading to her, sitting in their family room in a big chair that could hold both of them. Irene would read to her, first in Spanish and then in English, from a bilingual reader Irene had bought with her own money. Annie idolized Irene, and Irene had always been her protector, from the other girls' teasing and from kids in the neighborhood.

Her family had first discovered that Irene Salinas was not going to classes when they got a call from her high school. She had missed all three of her morning classes for two weeks and was only going to the other two, it seemed, because they came right after lunch and she liked to hang out with her friends at lunchtime. Her friends turned out to include some of the school's most active drug dealers, and Irene moved quickly from a little marijuana to some serious use of cocaine and Ecstasy. She began looking for the weekend parties where she knew drugs would be available, and had little trouble finding them.

Annie knew something was wrong, but in junior high she could only watch and wonder what Irene would do next. Next turned out to be getting arrested after a car full of drunk teenagers drove away from one of the parties and overturned at the next intersection. Irene had her seat belt on, but that didn't keep her out of juvenile hall when they found ten marijuana joints in her purse. After three months, Irene was released and immediately started bouncing from friends' couches to various crash pads around the neighborhood, until her parents finally said she couldn't come home unless she followed their rules about drug use and curfew.

She lived in a youth shelter, got arrested again, lived with a dealer who ended up beating her up, moved to a domestic violence shelter, and finally got kicked out of there when her drug use got so bad she stopped going to therapy.

So she was on the streets, and Annie by then was in college and had learned enough about Irene's lifestyle to know where to look for her. And so she looked, and two or three times when she found her, she almost wished she hadn't.

Irene's health had gone downhill very fast. She had gotten pneumonia from living outside in the rainy season, had been in and out of emergency rooms, and, Annie feared, was resorting to prostitution to cover her drug habit. She had found a place in a motel frequented by meth users, but ended up being evicted when the landlords caught her selling stolen property from her room.

Annie had spent many hours trying to figure out how Irene had gotten to be the way she was. Annie had known girls with severe drug problems whose parents were deeply religious non-drinkers, and she knew some that were fourth-generation alcoholics or addicts.

When she tried to trace Irene's problems back into her childhood, all she could remember was Irene as the center of attention, the special one, into whom her father and mother poured all their praise and rewards. Some of Annie's self-sufficiency came from growing up outside the glow of the spotlight on Irene. If Irene got an A, the world was sunny and bright. Later, when the goal was to get Irene simply to go to school, she was rewarded for just showing up. Annie's grades were very good, but the praise had faded as Irene's troubles had mounted up.

Annie's father was old school, a businessman who had started out with a small Mexican restaurant and had built it into a chain of seven profitable places. His business instincts were acute—but he left the girls to their mother, other than deciding who got how much allowance and later, who got how much help with college expenses. He was angered and bewildered by what had happened to Irene, and he left that to their mother, too.

But no matter what her parents did, Irene drifted away. Later, at college, Annie devoured everything she could find on the endless controversies about nature vs. nurture, trying to find the clue to how her parents had made Irene the way she was. Finally, she gave up, realizing that some unknowable mixture of tiny coils of DNA, things her parents had and had not done, and choices Irene had made herself had all forged the chute down which she plunged to her ruin.

The last time Annie had seen Irene was before she left to take the job at The Houses. She took Irene to a clean motel to let her take a shower and get a solid meal. Annie checked them in, left Irene in the shower, and went next door to a fast food place. When she came back with some burgers, fries and shakes, Irene was wrapped in a towel and was trying to wash her underwear in the sink. She finished, picked up a hairdryer, and began drying her underwear.

As she sat in a chair next to the bed where Irene was drying her clothes, Annie could see Irene's ribs and her gaunt and ravaged face. She tried not to react to seeing how much drugs and the street life had taken out of Irene's face and body. Irene threw her clothes back on and began wolfing down the food.

As she sat glaring at Annie, still sucking on the milkshake, Irene said "Don't look at me like you pity me, little Annie. I pity you, with your fancy college degree, going off to punch a time clock in some stupid job with a bunch of teenage brats."

Annie, who had learned most of her counseling skills the hard way, said only, "I hope I can see you when I come back to visit, Irene. I hope you're better, and I hope you get into treatment." And she reached forward and took Irene's skinny, scabbed-over hand, and said, "I love you, and I will find you wherever you are."

Irene began to cry softly, and said over and over, as she clumsily tried to put her skinny arms around Annie, "I'm sorry. I'm sorry for what I put you through. You're the only one who tried to help me—but I can't be helped any more, I'm just too far gone."

And then Annie let the anger out, putting her hands on Irene's shoulders and shaking her once, briefly. "Don't say that! You can get treatment—you know you have a disease and people much worse off than you have gotten well because they got into treatment and did the work."

Irene pulled away and looked out the window of the motel room. "Sure. Just go into some dump of a shelter and tell them my troubles and everything will be better."

Annie shook her head and said "You know that isn't what I mean. Some of the best programs in the country are here in Southern California, and you know you could get in if you wanted. But it's your call, Irene. You're the only one who can walk through that door."

Remembering, as the therapy group went on, more or less on automatic pilot, Annie knew she had done the clinically correct thing. Offer help, make a good referral to a good program, and then let the addict take the first step. But she often wondered if there was some other kind of motivation that would have worked—that would still work for Irene. She wondered about it every day.

Before she left to take the job with The Houses, her mother had taken her aside and said "Annie, I need to give you some advice, and I am not sure you are going to want it." She smiled, shrugged, and then said, "But I am going to give it to you anyway because I am your mother." She took Annie's face in her hands, and Annie could see she was about to cry. "I know you will be very good at this work. I just know it. But Annie, you must not let these girls become Irene to you. I know you have never given up on Irene, and I love you for it. But give these girls what you can because of what *they* need—not what Irene needs. Don't let them become Irene."

At the time, Annie wasn't sure she knew what her mother meant. Then, remembering how she'd snapped at Dolores, she had to admit that a lot of her feelings about Irene had been behind her anger. She decided she'd try to soften her approach to Dolores, starting with talking to her after the session.

10

Lexie

Since getting to Prospect, I had only had two explosions—but they were bad ones. They almost kicked me out for good in the first month, before I even got settled in. Sue and Sam and some of the staff would light my fuse with their stupid rules. They'd start in about how we were supposed to clean up and how to do it exactly right, and they would make you re-do it all over again if they didn't like it. And that would set me off, listening to them treat us like trash and order us around. And then I would grab something to get ready to throw it.

But the other girls had developed a kind of early warning system when somebody was going to blow up, and they would grab me before the staff did, and try to talk me down. Belinda was the best at it, because she was so damn big, and she could just wrap me up in her arms and walk me away from whatever was setting me off.

I had begun to feel that I was becoming part of the group, and then something would remind me that I wasn't yet. One afternoon after classes we were sitting around in the family room. Kendra, who was on duty, was on the phone. Whenever the girls had a chance to talk without staff listening, they loosened up a lot, and you could see how close some of them had become.

As they began trading stories, I could hear how much they shared that I had never tuned into. Quietly, they started telling stories about some funny stuff that had gone on before I got there.

"Girl, you remember the Scooters fight?"

"Oh yeah. They brought in that crappy old generic cereal, wannabe Cheerios, and they said we had to eat it. We went on a strike! That was so great."

"Wasn't too hard, because that was one of the days they had no milk."

"Right. Wal-Mart milk with expired dates was out of stock that week, so they couldn't even get sour milk for us. That was nasty!"

"Remember when they thought the landscaping crew outside was smoking weed and they made Kathy go outside and smell it? She went out, stood watching the guys work, took a few big breaths, held it in, and then came back in smiling saying, 'no, just tobacco.' But we knew, girl—we knew! She got herself some free weed."

"Remember when poor Dolores got a whole box of cookies from her mom and Sue snuck them into the apartment and ate every damn one of them?"

"That was mean—so cold and mean."

"Who remembers when we were off in Yellowstone for the big campout and Laurie decided to pierce her own belly button with a safety pin and screamed so loud she woke up the whole camp?"

They were all laughing so hard by now some of them had tears running down their faces.

"Oh, girl, I thought a wolf or mountain lion had got her and was chewing her ass up!"

"And remember the night we all set off the security alarms by throwing our slippers through the electronic detectors on the count of three! Totally pissed off the staff."

"And when the little old ladies from the senior center came by here with their packets of soap because they wanted to make sure we had good hygiene!"

"Yeah—they thought we were the dirty girls."

"And the time we got bored in therapy and we made up the story about how boys from the high school were sneaking into the other houses to diddle the girls?"

"They had armed guards out there all night long!"

I had been quiet, since these were all memories I hadn't been part of. But the last one was unbelievable. I asked, "You mean you make up things in therapy just to make it interesting?"

Belinda laughed her big hee-haw laugh. "All the time, girl. You think we want to listen to each other's sorry-ass stories about back home over and over? After you've been here for six months you know more than you ever want to about most of us. So we just make stuff up. Keeps it interesting."

By that time, Kendra had gotten off the phone and the volume of our conversation had gotten louder and louder. She walked over to where we were sitting on the couches and in her prim, tight-ass way she said, "Ladies, I do not believe those are stories that you need to tell. I heard some inappropriate words, so that will be 1000 negative points for all of you." When a chorus of no's resulted, she quickly said "And 1000 more if you don't accept your consequences without arguing. Don't any of you have homework from classes today?"

Kendra was one of the three regular staff who were on in the daytime, in addition to Sue and Sam, the house parents. Evelyn and the head staff person, Annie, were the other two. They were as different from each other as the girls were, and I was getting to know more and more about their weird little game-playing and which ones could sometimes be OK.

Kendra was the worst, then Evelyn, then Sue. Annie was the best. They could all be total tight-asses when they wanted, but Kendra never let up. She seemed mad all the time, and really hated her job. A few months ago she had told one of the girls "I hate every minute I am with you little brats, and I'm just counting the days until I can go back to school." Of course everyone repeated the remark over and over, and it made her one of the prime targets any time we got some kind of prank going. She had a high, kind of sing-song voice. We called her Miss Priss.

Evelyn was just plain bossy. She got off on giving us orders, and was at her worst on the weekends when she supervised what they called "deep cleans," which was when we had to clean everything in the house from our rooms to the kitchen, the utility room, and the classrooms. Everybody hated deep clean days, but when Evelyn was on, it was much worse. She rubbed her finger along the window ledges to see if they were "really clean." And she would go in the utility room where the washer and dryer were and pull the machines out from the wall to make sure we cleaned the lint behind them. She was short, and always used her middle finger to check our deep cleans, so we called her the Digit Midget.

One Saturday during deep cleans Belinda found a dead mouse outside the house and put it behind the washer. We all waited out in the hall for Evelyn's scream—which almost broke the windows.

Sue was the quiet one, and you could never tell just what she was going to do. Some days she was friendly, and some days she was a PITA—a total pain in the ass. We called her Rita Pita. But she could be totally cool—one time she took us to a drive-in and let us get up on top of the van with a ton of candy to watch the movie. Then she would take points away when it made no sense. Monica once said she thought they all had a quota, like cops when they write traffic tickets, and had to give a certain number of point takeaways in a week to show they were doing their job. But Sue was random when she did it, and most of us steered clear of her whenever we could.

Even though he was a houseparent, Sam had much less to do with the girls. He was going to school part-time, and he did the ordering and shopping for the house on a computer in the staff office.

There was a part-timer, Lorraine somebody, who was a student and just came in during afternoons and evenings. I didn't know much about her, though the other girls said she was an easier grader on points than the other staff.

Annie was usually mellow, and because she had been there the longest and got to know us through her therapy sessions, she was a lot more understanding when one of us was having a bad day. After I got to know her better, she opened up a little about having a sister who was bipolar and hooked on drugs. I could tell that she knew a lot more about who we were than the rest of the staff did.

Dr. Gustafson, the shrink—he was really a psychologist, not a psychiatrist—who came to see us once a week, was hard to figure out. He was tall, and mostly bald, and asked us questions like he was reading them from a list. "Well, how are we feeling today?" 'How are you getting along with the other girls?" He sometimes asked us "What would you like to talk about today?" and then was quiet until we answered him. I usually said "Getting home," to which his answer was always "And what are you doing to make that happen?" It got to be like a tennis match or ping-pong game—he'd ask something, I'd answer, he'd ask something else, and it went on and on. I never got the feeling that he knew much about us or had worked much with girls with our problems. He had his list of questions, we recited our own list of answers—and nothing really made any difference. We called him Dr. Chromedome.

Dealing with all these staff people in the house was a huge pain. It was like they were each on different wave lengths, and you had to be careful to use the right approach with each of them. What would work with one of them was a total mistake with one of the others. I felt like I was trying to put together a puzzle and they kept changing the shape of the pieces all the time.

Belinda had told me early on that Laurie was the champion at getting the staff to blow up, and I saw it happen several times. She had this way of quietly defying them whenever they told her to do something she didn't want to do—she was amazing. Without ever confronting them, she could make them lose control.

Annie told me one time in therapy that girls who do that have a thing where they get a sort of natural high when they can make other people explode—because then it seems like they're the ones in control. Annie said it was about their own anger and trying to get other people to lose it so they didn't have to deal with their own stuff.

I couldn't do it—I blew up faster than most people. But Laurie could go back and forth and make it sound like she was the most reasonable person in the world and the staff person was nuts.

She did it one Saturday with Kendra, after Kendra had asked us to re-do our deep cleans. We had kind of slopped out the work because we wanted to go watch a soccer game in Desert City, and after she checked it, Kendra told us to do everything over. And then Laurie asked her how she could do her job better this time.

"Laurie, stop arguing."

"I know that I shouldn't be arguing and I really don't mean to. But I don't think that's what I'm doing, Kendra. I just want to make sure I understand what you want us to do."

Part of it was her tone. Laurie had a level, quiet voice and so she never seemed like she was losing it by raising her voice.

"Just do the work, Laurie, or I'm going to give you negatives for arguing."

"I really don't mean to argue. Kendra. I agree that I need to do the job over, and I totally accept that. But could you please tell me what parts of the job need the most improvement? I really want to get it right this time."

"The whole damned thing, Laurie. Do it all over—and stop bugging me!" Staff were never supposed to swear at us, so Laurie had already won on points by getting Kendra to yell and getting her to swear.

"OK, Kendra. I'm sorry I bothered you." Again, all in the quietest, meekest little voice you ever heard.

We knew it wasn't how we were supposed to handle staff, but we had so little control over what they did to us, it was pure joy sometimes to watch someone on our side of the fence who could get them to lose it. Laurie was our champion.

They had this thing at The Houses called "peer reporting" where you could get negatives because some other girl would rat you out and tell when you had broken a rule. It meant that whenever somebody new came into the house we all acted fake for a while until we figured out whether she was going to peer report us. I hated it because it meant you couldn't really trust anybody. The program was supposed to be about helping us to have normal friendships, and then they set up this stupid thing where everyone was encouraged to rat everybody else out. Most of the girls got to where they wouldn't do it, but sometimes somebody would get mad at another girl, and then you had to watch what you said around them because they would peer report you.

11

Annie: A week later

Annie had a second therapy session coming up with Lexie, and decided to call Lexie's mother in advance, to try to fill in some of the background. Annie started the conversation by explaining the call.

"Mrs. Crockett, it would help me a lot in talking with Lexie if you could tell me how you and Mr. Crockett see her. I've got the files, and the testing, and a lot of paper. But parents sometimes can add a lot to the paper that piles up."

Annie could hear a long pause that her skilled ear picked up as likely to be Mrs. Crockett trying to get control of herself before she began. "Ms. Salinas . . ."

"Annie—Annie is fine."

"Annie, OK. Let me see if I can help you here. You'll have to excuse me, we're having a tough time with her gone and . . ." she stopped and Annie heard a sob being cut off. ". . . and we're trying to handle it as best we can. It's so hard having her gone, but . . ." she paused again, and then her words rushed forward. "But in a way it's a relief to know she's safe there for now and that we're not worried about whether she is in a hospital some place—or worse."

She was quiet and then she said "This may sound awful, but Lexie can be very convincing in rationalizing whatever she wants to do. She's verbally very smooth and manipulative. She's not there with you because she cuts school or sneaks out of the house, or ignores our rules about what she needs to do to help out around the house. She's there because what she was doing when she went out of control seemed to be getting more and more dangerous."

She laughed, with a very sad undertone, Annie thought, and went on. "Lexie said it best herself one day when she was fairly calm and was explaining herself to us. She said 'I just feel like I've got no brakes—nothing holds me back once I get an idea in my head.'"

Mrs. Crockett continued. "Now we've talked to the clinicians at school and her psychiatrist and we've read all the books they recommended and we know all about executive functioning and the prefrontal cortex and all that. And we've tried six different prescriptions and combinations of meds, off and on since she was ten years old." She laughed. "If I'd known I was going to be handling all these drugs, I'd have majored in chemistry in college instead of design. Or accounting—to deal with all the insurance.

"It just got more and more frightening to us. She'd sneak out of the house after we went to sleep and then come back the next afternoon. Then it escalated and she'd stay out two or three nights, and she wouldn't answer her cellphone. So we took it away and then we had no way to reach her when she'd disappear.

"We spent thousands and thousands of dollars alarming the house and the yard. But she'd just wait until we were asleep and get out of the house and into someone's car within seconds after the alarm went off. It never stopped her."

"We've both been very busy, Ted with his accounting practice and I've worked a lot in home decorating and now in politics." She laughed, but not happily. "Lexie thinks the politics is just socializing, but I really care about some of the issues that some people in Congress are trying to push. Some of it is about kids with mental illnesses like Lexie's." She trailed off and was quiet for a moment. "But Lexie sees us as preoccupied with our business. No matter how much time we gave her, she seemed to notice when we were busy more than when we were focused on her."

"Was she sexually active, Mrs. Crockett?"

"She had plenty of opportunity to be—but I don't think she was really out of control there. From what my friends say, all the girls have 'done it.' But only a few are totally impulsive about sex. Then we got lucky, I guess, although Lexie's friend, who got a terrible STD and was hospitalized, wasn't so lucky. But Lexie got really scared by that, and talked to me after that happened. And I think that slowed her down a bit. At least I hope so.

"When she ran, we'd call the cops and they'd come to the house and take down all the details about her friends and where she might be staying. But after four or five times, you could see that the police had given up—on her and on us, both. They saw she was still coming home and they saw that we had less and less control over her. And when she'd finally come home, they'd send out an officer, and she'd talk to Lexie, trying to scold her enough about violating curfew so that she'd take it seriously. But she never really did."

Annie waited to see if there was more. Then she said, quietly, "It must have been very hard on you and Mr. Crockett."

This time Annie heard the sob. "Thank you, Annie. You have no idea how much that means, and how rare it is for someone to say that to us."

Annie said, "We'll do everything we can here, Mrs. Crockett. But I know you know that Lexie has to do the hard work here by herself. We can't do it for her—we can help her, and you and Mr. Crockett can help her. But it's finally up to her. She's fifteen, and she'll be eighteen in no time and then she goes into the adult system. And then it's totally different, because the second chances are over."

"I know, I know. And we still have a lot of hope. We've liked what we've heard about your program, and we're looking forward to visiting in two weeks."

As Annie hung up, she wondered whether it would do any good to discuss Lexie with Jerome Jolson, the consulting psychiatrist from the university. Some of the things her mother had said seemed to point toward a need for even stronger impulse control medications, and she pulled out her file to review what Lexie was currently taking.

Annie had heard staff call Dr. Jolson "the drive by shrink," and the first time she saw him "assess" four girls in less than two hours, she knew what they meant. Jolson was short, and Annie read him as one of those short guys who was constantly trying to make up for it by being overbearing. It usually came out a few shades short of totally obnoxious. He only saw girls once a month, which Annie thought was ridiculous. He rarely consulted with Annie or Gustafson, despite their more frequent contacts with the girls, preferring to rely on his own "diagnosis." Most of the girls in Prospect had simple medication regimens. But Annie had heard more than one story from counselors in other houses that Jolson had taken some of their girls off meds entirely, with disastrous results. As she thought about it, she reluctantly shelved the idea of consulting Jolson, at least for the time being.

12

Annie; Two weeks later

Parents' meeting weekend was held by The Houses staff every three months with as many parents as could attend. Annie entered the conference room in the classroom building and sat down, smiling at the group that had assembled. They were sitting around the big table, with most of the parents on one side of the table, which meant that staff had to sit on the other side. Annie always felt like the seating arrangement set up a troubling us-them dynamic, but her suggestions for changes had been politely dismissed by senior staff.

Annie's role in these meetings, it had been made clear to her early in her work at The Houses, was to listen. The meeting was run by Suzanne Ellison, the program director of The Houses. She was a trim, tall woman in her late forties who entered the room carrying a clipboard and dressed in a business suit.

"Excuse my formal outfit," she began. "I just came from a meeting at our headquarters offices in Desert City." She looked around the group of ten parents, four couples and two single moms who sat slightly apart from the others. "Why don't we begin by telling each other who your daughters are and a little about ourselves, so we can get to know each other?"

As Annie listened to the parents go around the table, she was struck once again at the wide variation in the girls' families. The Houses accepted a mixture of "public girls," meaning those referred from state or county mental health, probation, and child welfare agencies, and "private girls," many of whom were fully paid for by parents who could afford the high fees. No one was supposed to know which girls were which—but everyone did.

Annie had attended several of the parents' meetings over the years, and the pattern was nearly always the same. The meetings were described in the invitation letter as an "opportunity to share your reactions to our program and provide us with valuable feedback, since parents are vital stakeholders in our system of care."

But "the program," Annie gradually saw, was rarely what the group talked about. Most of the parents needed air time to complain about how hard it was to raise these girls. And the staff happily let the group talk about the parents' problems rather than anything that might be wrong with the agency or its programs. And Annie came to feel that the parents who never showed—either because they were from too far away, couldn't afford to come, or didn't give a damn—were the parents the staff needed most to try to reach.

One of the mothers edged forward in her chair. She was well-dressed and had carefully sculptured hair. She began speaking in a soft voice. "I'd like to talk about coping strategies. Ours, I mean—not the girls'. How do the rest of you deal with having your daughter here?" She stopped, blinked away some tears, and went on, "The other day I broke down driving by a soccer game back home. Just a simple soccer game out on the field at our neighborhood school. It was so peaceful, a kind of peace we haven't had in our family for six years. Kids playing, parents watching. So different from our family."

Her husband reached over and took her hand. "Normies, our kids call them. The normal kids who would never dream of acting out. Normies. It took me a long time, but I can now listen to friends at dinner and read their Facebook pages talking about their kids' SAT scores and getting into Ivy League schools without getting enraged at them. They just have no clue what it's like to realize that high school graduation is the real academic finish line. And she may not even make that."

One of the other mothers nodded and spoke up. "Dropping your little girl off at a strange place and driving away. That's about as low as I've been. Losing her, having her die, would be worse, I know, but having to put her somewhere out here where she doesn't want to be, and driving away—that's as sad as I think I've ever been. You drive a mile or so and then you're on this narrow country road out there—" she motioned to the road that ran past The Houses, "and you're crying so hard you can't see anything, and so you pull over and you just cry and cry for a long time. And then you start the car and drive to the airport to fly home, and she's left back there. And day by day, you hear her on the phone, sad, then adjusting a little, then happy about something, then sad again, and then she starts crying and says I want to come home and you have to say no. It is the hardest thing I ever did. You agree that you will send this beautiful, gifted, chaotic child you have loved for fifteen years to a place where she may get better but where she will hate you for part of every day because you sent her there."

She was choking up, and her husband was patting her on the shoulder, but she went on. "It's hard duty, this parenting stuff. And when I hear parents complaining about how much first-rate colleges cost, I want to scream at them 'do you have any bloody idea just how lucky you are?'" She choked up and could not go on.

Her husband patted her hand again, and then began talking, looking at Annie and Suzanne. "You people work very hard and I really appreciate what you do. I really do. But I don't think any of you can ever understand what it is like to be a parent and to try . . ." he stopped, struggling for control, "to try to do everything we can for our daughter." He stopped again, wiping his eyes. "We have to put up with things most parents would never tolerate—that our parents would have been horrified to see if we had ever dared to do it to them. They swear at us, they hit us, they spit at us, they tell us they hate us and hope we will die."

Annie could see other parents nodding, sad-faced. "And an hour later they say they're sorry. And they are a joy to be with—and then something sets them off and the cycle begins all over again."

He pointed to the books they had been given. "Give them limits, they tell us. Those parenting books, they talk about giving them limits. They never tell you where those limits are supposed to stop, though. And she still blames us! We've told her over and over that we've lost control of what happens to her, because the law and the judges take over after you cross too many lines. But she still blames us."

He had calmed down, and was talking more slowly. "You know, I never understood Christianity and that 'other cheek' stuff until I got hit in the face by my daughter and had to stand there and let her hit me again, because she was so angry, so lost and out of control, that all I could do was hope she would wake up from her rage and see what she was doing.

"It's so hard to find the balance in holding them accountable—to teach them that they will be judged for their actions, regardless of their disabilities. When do you forgive them and blame the disorder for the behavior? When do you blame them because they chose to do it, and you know damn well that they sometimes hide behind the disease? And we read about your behavior modification program," he gestured toward Suzanne, "but we know it's not as simple as them choosing to behave that way. You never know—and you're always looking for the place where you draw that line."

And a mother said *Yes* under her breath, but loud enough that she could be heard by everyone in the room.

At this point Annie noticed that most of the parents were listening, some of them clearly getting ready to tell their own stories. But one of the fathers, leaning back in hopes that he would not be too obvious, moved his jacket up his sleeve and took a look at his watch. He had mentioned to Suzanne as he came in that he would have to leave early to go to a meeting.

Another mother spoke up in a very calm, controlled voice, and said "We believe it's all in God's hands. We have our whole church praying for our daughter. But it's all in God's hands." The looks she got from the others ranged from soft nods to stares of incredulity.

A woman dressed very plainly in a print dress began talking hesitantly in a very soft voice, looking down at the floor, not making eye contact with any of them. "When we got home from dropping her off, we turned on the radio just to get some sound in the house. It was so quiet with her gone. And this song came on, with Linda Ronstadt singing it, I think. It was the "Somewhere Out There" song from the Fievel movie, *American Tail*. Laurie liked that movie a lot when she was little, and we started listening to the words. It's about . . ." she put her head in her hands, shuddered, and then got herself back under control. "It's about somewhere out there, someone's thinking of you and loving you . . ." but by then she was crying so much, she couldn't go on any further. Annie noticed that some of the parents were wiping their eyes, while a few were watching impassively as if they didn't want to get involved in all that emotion.

A father cleared his throat and began talking. "I'd like to talk about how hard it is to get straight answers from the bureaucracies we have to deal with. My wife and I both have master's degrees, and we've worked with bureaucracies and court systems all our professional lives. And most of the time we're totally confused about how to make this work. At one point my wife was negotiating with people in three different states about the Medicaid benefits our daughter was entitled to because she's a special needs adopted child. And none of those people understood how the other states' systems worked for girls who were moved across state lines by decisions made by county agencies and school districts. And after all that, we still had to negotiate with our own insurance company—which had no idea how Medicaid worked."

A mother sitting next to him nodded and said, "I went to a conference of adoptive parents last year and there was a Supreme Court Justice from another state who had adopted a girl. And he talked about how the school district and the state agency in his own state had hassled him in getting educational benefits for his daughter—benefits that he knew she was entitled to get. A Supreme Court Justice! If people like that and people like us are having trouble—what happens to the average parent who comes up against that kind of hassling?"

The father who had begun the topic, whom Annie now recognized as Lexie Crockett's father, Ted, answered. "They give up, and the bureaucracy wins. Or the people running the program win, because parents have no idea how to appeal, or they get frightened that it will cost them huge amounts of time and money if they disagree with anything the agency decides."

The session went on for a half hour or so, with parents continuing to talk about their own responses to their girls' problems. Then a very professional-looking mother in a business suit cleared her throat and asked Suzanne, "I'd be interested in knowing what your metrics are here." Seeing the puzzled expression on Suzanne's face, she added, impatiently, "I mean how do you measure progress? What are the benchmarks you use to determine when these girls are ready to go home?"

Suzanne smiled, and answered, "That's why we have the levels system. As was explained in the packet we gave you when your daughter enrolled here, we use a points system of incentives to reward our girls for positive behavior. As they accumulate points and meet our expectations, we move them through the four levels of the program. At level 4, we begin exit planning with the parents and your school districts . . ." she paused, "or private schools of your choice, to transition the girls back into the schools they came from."

As Annie watched, it was obvious that this particular mother wasn't buying it. "So these levels depend on how your staff rate the girls? But what are the standards for the ratings—what prevents a staff member from taking points away from a girl just because she doesn't like her, or because the girl disagrees with what she has been asked to do?" She stopped, and then plunged ahead. "My daughter told me, for example, that one of the staff called her a spoiled bitch and said she would take points away from her every time she got a chance. Where are the standards in all that?"

Suzanne kept the smile. "I'm sure you understand that sometimes our girls—" Annie could hear the careful use of our girls rather than your daughter—"may misinterpret what someone has said to them. But if you'll just let Annie know after the meeting which staff person was involved, we'll look into it and get back to you."

"Well, now let me understand how that would work. You'll have Annie ask the staff person if she said it and she'll say no, and my daughter will say yes. Then what?"

Unfortunately for the mother, the other parents were by this time acting as if they felt she was monopolizing their time with her complaint. "I wonder if we can get back on track here," said the father who had mentioned that he had another meeting, looking at his watch again.

Sensing that she had gained the momentum back, Suzanne said, "Thank you for sharing your concern with us. Now are there any other questions?"

An older father, balding and a bit overweight, who had said nothing in the meeting raised his hand politely and asked with a faint smile, "You mentioned meeting at your headquarters office. Do you mind my asking who owns this organization?"

Suzanne frowned. "Who owns it? The Houses is a nonprofit organization that has operated this program for the past twenty years."

"Yes, I understand that. That doesn't answer my question, though. Who owns the nonprofit? Who runs the parent company and who benefits from its income?" The father had stopped smiling.

Suzanne answered with a pained look, "Actually, at the moment we are going through an ownership change, and until those negotiations are completed, I'm not at liberty to answer that question."

"Fine, I can understand that. But can I assume the ownership change, when it is consummated, will be announced to the parents and agencies who are paying for the program?"

Suzanne's expression was even more pained, although Annie could see she was struggling to keep from revealing the full depth of her irritation. "I would imagine that would be the case. But the new owners, if indeed they complete the transaction, will make that decision."

The father was not backing off, and Annie wondered what he was really driving at. He went on, "I understand that you personally would not make that decision. Who should we be in touch with at the central office to find out who would be making that decision?"

Annie noticed by that time that he had used the code phrase "I understand" three times. She recalled a conversation she had with one of the girls a few weeks ago in one of the therapy sessions. The girl had angrily said, "You guys have this stupid phrase you say over and over when any of us ask a question or show that we're pissed off about your silly rules. You all say 'I understand how you are feeling.' But you're not us—you're not locked up here a thousand miles away from home. You get up and walk out of here and go home to your nice apartment every day. So how do you get off telling us you understand?!"

Annie wondered if this father had deliberately used the phrase to bait Suzanne or if he was just trying to seem reasonable, to take the edge off his persistence in questioning Suzanne.

Suzanne by that time had also heard the phrase and assumed that he was using it deliberately. She decided to end it. "I'll pass along your concern to the central office."

The father had also decided the usefulness of the exchange was over. "Thanks," he said with the same faint smile he wore as he began his questioning.

Annie wondered what the exchange had been about. She had heard rumors about The Houses possibly being bought by some big company, but she knew nothing more than the vague rumors. She made a mental note to ask Monica, whose father had raised the issue, what her father did for a living. She wondered if he had a way of learning about companies buying other companies.

As they were leaving the meeting, two of the mothers who had attended the meeting without their husbands asked Annie if they could talk to her. Annie took them into an alcove off the main lobby of the classroom building where the meeting had been held.

"Could we talk to you for a minute? We didn't want to say anything at the meeting, but we really needed some advice. We don't get a lot of what is being talked about in there. We commute over from Desert City—we don't have as far to come as some of them, but we have to take time off from work and so it's not easy to get here. And we wondered if you could . . ." she was trying to ask something that was embarrassing her, Annie could see, and she tried to help her.

"Give you some advice?"

"Yes, sort of."

Then the mother who hadn't spoken yet said, in a voice even more tentative than her friend, "We really don't know when we should speak up, even though we think some of what is happening to our daughters is not right. All you people have all those degrees and training and all that—and we're just not sure if we should disagree with anything. And so we thought maybe we could talk to you."

Annie smiled at them and said, "Nobody knows your daughters as well as you do. If you're here, you're doing it because you want your daughters to get better. And that entitles you to speak up any time you want. Ask any questions you want. We have the responsibility to explain it clearly—you don't have to understand all our jargon and professional labels."

The younger woman stepped forward and shook Annie's hand, pumping it as she spoke. "Thank you, that's what we hoped you would say. Thank you so much."

Annie's sisters, Beatrice and Geraldine, were both working in social services programs back home in Orange County. Bea was a counselor at a drug and alcohol treatment program, and Gerry had worked in a domestic violence shelter for ten years. Annie knew there was no big mystery why they had ended up in programs like that. But it meant that they understood a lot of what Annie was dealing with, and since both of them still saw her as the "little sister," they were good about staying in touch and often sent her chatty emails.

Over time, in her work at The Houses, Annie had come to use her emails to her sisters as a way of thinking about what was happening in her work and how she felt about it. She liked being able to write to two people who knew her intimately and would call her on any "thinking errors"—which was the phrase used in The Houses to refer to the girls' sometimes confused logic.

Email
From: Annie Salinas to Beatrice Salinas
Subject: Parents

I know you work with parents a lot in your programs, and so do we. Today we had a session that made me think a lot about Irene—and about Mom and Dad. We had some parents here for a meeting, and you could see that some of them are trying as hard as they can to understand what is happening to their daughters. And others sit there and make clear that they don't give a damn. And the ones we most need to make contact with never even come here for a parents' meeting.

Parents are both the problem and the solution here—they can help their girls enormously, or they can pressure them so hard that they break. And some of them will just ignore them until they make trouble—and then they send them to us to get "fixed."

I wish we had a really good parental competency test that was as good as the drug tests you guys use. Except that I'd be afraid that more than half of our parents would fail it.

Love you,
Annie

13

Lexie

Annie and Dr. Gustafson are always trying to get me to talk about my parents in therapy. My parents aren't terrible. And I don't think they're terrible—they just don't get it.

Although after listening to some of these girls' stories in therapy, I'm beginning to think parents who don't get it are a whole hell of a lot better than parents who are total assholes. Some of these kids' parents just dumped them here to get them out of the house. One girl won't take calls from her father anymore because every time he calls he's totally drunk, or high on some pills he takes, and she just decided nothing he ever says makes sense when he's like that, so why talk to him?

A few of the girls won't even talk about their parents in group because they abused them or beat them up or something awful. The girls who were here before told us a story about one girl who lived at The Houses a few years ago. The way Monica heard the story from a girl who was just leaving here when Monica got here a year ago, "she finally worked out after all that therapy that it wasn't her fault she was abused. Then she figured out whose fault it was, and when she got home—she killed him."

So I guess I don't have the worst parents, even if they are clueless sometimes. After my parents came to visit the first time, one of the quiet girls came up to me and said "Can I adopt your parents?" I think it was only partly a joke.

My dad is an accountant, and he works with numbers all the time, and he likes things to be neat and precise. Which I am not. So I bug him, and he bugs me. Though he can be very generous and even funny sometimes—for an accountant. We watch movies together sometimes, and he relaxes, and can be a lot of fun.

My mom, Angela, works part-time for a design firm that decorates houses. She's really good at it, and makes enough money that she only works part-time so she can be at home with me and my sister. That's what she tells people, anyway. But she's not really home that much because she does a lot of social things with women's groups and political stuff. We live in Orange, in a big house my mom decorated.

And then there's my sister Justine. "The good one," people call her, in comparison to me. She's 19, and she goes to college, and she's blond and sort of cheerleader cute—all of which I am not. Somebody told me I have "smoky looks" which I guess means dark and not as happy-faced as my sister. We used to get along and then she got really popular in high school and I was still in middle school. And she kind of left me behind, and we just didn't have that much to do with each other from then on.

The last time we tried family therapy as a whole family, after I had run away for four days and gotten arrested, Justine sat and said nothing for an hour or so. Finally the therapist turned to her and said "Justine, what do you think about Lexie's role in the family?"

And Justine just looked at her and then said "I am so sick and tired of all this talk about Lexie and her problems. She just needs to get over it and get a life." And then she walked out and waited in the car until we were done.

Thanks, sister.

A new girl had just arrived with the same escort service that brought me—I recognized the driver. They came in and stopped in the front hallway. The girl had a brown duffel bag and stood watching as Sam completed the paperwork to sign her in.

Then the escort left, and Sam said to the three of us who had come out in the hallway, "This is Sophia, and she'll be living here with us."

We went up and introduced ourselves. This was a big part of the house ritual—you were supposed to introduce yourself to anyone who came into the house and offer to shake hands with them.

Sophia was short, about three inches shorter than me, and had sort of blonde hair that looked like it had been cut by someone who should never have been allowed to touch scissors. It was hacked off in uneven lengths, and just hung straight down, no more than three or four inches. She was frowning, glaring at us really, but you could see she would be semi-good looking if she ever stopped frowning. She just muttered "Hi" when Sam introduced her, not looking at us.

Sam took her upstairs to show her the room she would be sharing with Laurie, and the rest of us stood around for a minute trying to figure her out.

"What a snob," Amanda said.

"We were all like that when we first got here," I said. "Maybe she'll loosen up."

In the first few weeks I was at Prospect, Belinda told me some things about her growing up in Kentucky that helped me understand her a little bit better. She said she had been much closer to her father than her mother. Her father had never done the "girlie stuff" with her. Her mother was into riding and trading horses and was often away at races and shows. So Belinda spent a lot of time with her father, who had encouraged her in whatever she wanted to do.

"When I turned thirteen, I shot up to six feet tall. So I thought I wanted to be a model." She laughed. "Me—Hulk Hogan's sister—a model. But Dad loved the idea and sent me to a summer school where I learned all this hairdressing stuff. Then I just got bigger and bigger—not tall, just big." She flexed her huge arms and looked fierce, then laughed. "And so he said maybe I could model for weightlifting magazines."

Her voice cracked, and she said "He could always make me laugh." She went on, trying not to show her emotion. "He loved Western movies—"

"Really? My dad too—he's a fanatic."

"Same here. He had a collection of hundreds of them—the old oaters made out in this place in California called the Alabama Hills, and all the new ones too. He knew lines from all of them."

"My dad too! He made me and my sister watch the ones he said were the best ones—*Stagecoach, Silverado, Pale Rider, The Cowboys*. His favorite was *The Magnificent Seven . . .*"

Belinda got this weird look on her face and said in a low, tough voice, "We deal in lead, friend."

And I immediately answered her "Sometimes you have to turn mother's picture to the wall and ride on down that road."

Then it was Belinda's turn. "You elected?"

I pretended to pull a cigar out of my mouth and look at the end of it. "No, but I got nominated real good."

We cracked up laughing, falling back on the couch where we were sitting. Belinda said "Girls watching Westerns. Boy, are we weird."

"Yeah—the misfits."

Then she got a sad look on her face, and said "He approved of almost anything I wanted to do that wasn't illegal. He used to walk around the house singing in a terrible, off-key voice the same silly line from Home on the Range: Where seldom is heard, a discouraging word, and the skies are not cloudy all day." She was quiet. Then she said, "And he lived it, too. He never discouraged me."

I waited a moment, and then asked, "What happened?"

She looked off through the window at the fences outside the house. "He died when I was fourteen. Heart attack." She was quiet for a long time, and I waited. "Then my mother, who had no clue whatsoever what to do with me, decided to send me off to my father's sister to live there, in Virginia. She had a job and older kids, and didn't much care what I did. So I started running around loose, and ended up with the usual booze, drugs, and sex crowd. Two abortions later, I got arrested for shoplifting and the county sent me here."

She was quiet for a long time. Then she looked straight at me and said, "You know you're lucky, Lexie. You know that, right?"

"I guess."

"Don't guess!" She sounded angry. "From all I can tell, you have two parents who give a damn. And that's one or two more than the rest of us." She grabbed her hair bag, full of all her curling irons and straightening irons and hair gel and sprays. "C'mon, let's braid your hair."

She'd dropped the subject, but I couldn't. In a way, it was more therapy than I'd gotten in all the time I'd been at The Houses. Seeing my parents through someone else's eyes was a different way of thinking about them. And it really made me think about how rotten I treated my parents sometimes.

14

Annie

Lexie was still on the edge—she had exploded a few times, but the other girls had rescued her from going too far. When Annie talked to her about it, Lexie would clam up and mutter "I don't know" when Annie asked her why she thought she had lost control.

Lexie's mother had said that Lexie admitted that she had "bad brakes," an unscientific term Annie had heard before after a lot of reading on executive functioning—the part of the brain that says *this is really not a good idea so don't do it*. Some of these girls' brains simply lacked the connections to over-ride their impulses. Annie had read that this was true of all adolescents, but these girls often had even worse executive functioning than most of their peers, as a result of trauma or prenatal drug or alcohol exposure.

Lexie was a frowner, whose face often dropped into a sullen, shut-down mask when she was in a group or a one-on-one with Annie. Then after a while, she would go to a blank stare, and Annie sometimes wondered whether she had fallen into a trance. In their early sessions, Annie had counted it a huge victory when she occasionally got Lexie to break out a tiny smile, revealing a perfect dimple that softened her face into an almost welcoming look. Annie knew there was something buried well beneath the frown, and knew it was her job to figure out what it was.

Annie hated the label "oppositional defiant" because she had seen therapists and staff use it as a lazy way of saying "the kid won't do what I tell her to." In Annie's view, this labeling often concealed the staff's own mistakes in giving inconsistent, too-rapid commands to girls with auditory processing problems. Time after time, Annie had seen it: sometimes a girl who doesn't absorb a request the first time she hears it isn't being oppositional—she's still trying to figure out what you want, or she's already forgotten it. And then, under pressure because she didn't comply immediately, she explodes.

At the same time, Annie thought as she watched Lexie sulk, there was also a kind of reckless behavior that some of the girls adopted as a pose, especially when they had been rejected by peers. *You don't like me, fine—watch what crazy-ass stuff I can do* was how Annie sometimes decoded their behavior.

Of course, telling a kid to do something she doesn't want to do—or telling her no when she asks for something—is part of life. And Annie had more than a bit of sympathy for new staff who would come in and encounter this refusal behavior and look at Annie as if to say who do these girls think they are—princesses?!

So Annie decided to take a risk.

The rules said that girls could not be let off campus until they had completed the first month of the program. Annie had worked out a three-mile run that was partly on the property and then looped up into the foothills before it came back to property owned by The Houses. She checked with Deborah Wong, the site supervisor who reported to Suzanne Ellison, and Deborah, after calling the central office, said on a one-time basis Annie would be allowed to let Lexie run with her on the three-mile route.

The next morning, Annie took Lexie aside as she was leaving for classes, and asked her "Lexie, do you want to go for a run this afternoon after class?"

Lexie was surprised and gave a quick answer, "Sure, why not?"

So that afternoon Lexie came back from her last class, changed into her sneakers, and met Annie out front where she was stretching out. Lexie had a pair of jeans on and a T-shirt from her former high school in Orange. Annie wore a Cal State Fullerton cross-country sweat shirt.

Annie started off at a slow pace, and Lexie had no difficulty keeping up with her. After they left The Houses property, the trail began to go up toward the foothills more steeply, and Annie could tell that Lexie was starting to labor a bit. But she had a long stride, and Annie guessed that she had been a good runner in competition.

"When did you last run?" Annie asked her.

"Oh, a few weeks ago, before I went to the hospital." Lexie was breathing hard, but kept a step or two ahead of Annie so that Annie could see she didn't want her to ease up.

They kept going up for another mile or so, and then the trail curved off to the north and they stopped at the top. They were high enough that they could see thirty miles or so out into the vast desert to the west. Lexie had not seen it yet, and she stared out at the horizon as they caught their breath before starting on the downhill part. The sunset was beginning, and there were pinkish streaks rising from the far-off edge of the desert.

"Wow. That's a view."

"Sure is. I like coming up here just to see where we are."

They headed on down the hill and finished the run with a half-sprint. As they leaned on the fence up against the front of the house, getting their breath, Lexie said, puffing hard, "Thanks. That felt great."

"You're welcome. We can do it again if you want."

"For sure."

15

Lexie

MAY

Then my parents visited. It was the second time that they had been here, but I only got to see them for a brief visit the first time they came.

I wondered how they were going to take my being in this new place, even though they agreed to it. Sometimes I didn't have a clue how to talk to them.

My dad does this thing where he gets fed up with my backtalk or my refusing to do what he wants me to, and he just snaps. He says "Fine, then there's no need to talk about it anymore." And then he walks away, which makes me snap.

My mom is much better at talking things out, but sometimes I just wish she would drop it. She has much more patience than my dad, and is better at talking to me. She never walks away—even when I wish she would because we've talked something to death.

My parents were going to meet with staff and then we were all supposed to have "family therapy." Oh joy . . .

They came in about 10 in the morning—I had to get out of class, which was fine with me. They hugged me in the front hallway, with staff there, quickly swarming my parents, all over them. Finally I had a chance to talk to them without anybody else around. We sat in the fancy room, with me in an armchair, and them on the couch

"How do you like it, Lexie?" asked my mom.

"I hate it—what do you expect?"

"Tell us why you hate it." That's my dad—Mr. Rational. Except when he gets mad and goes all OIC—that means out of instructional control here. It's code for blowing up.

"The staff treats us like crap, the food sucks, the therapy is a joke, and I'm getting nothing out of it."

My dad got the look he always gets when I tell him something he doesn't want to hear. My mom said, "Is there anything you like about it? Anything at all?"

"Sure," I said. "The fact that I can get out of here in six months."

"Not if you don't do the work," my dad said.

Just what I wanted to hear. "I'll do the work. But I don't have to like it."

My dad said, "Lexie, your attitude is part of what determines whether they move you up in the levels. You know that—they explained it to you, and we've kept saying it when we talk to you on the phone."

Then my mom changed the subject. "We heard from staff that you had a run yesterday. How was that?"

"It was pretty good. The trail wasn't much but it was cool to get a little ways up into the hills." I laughed. "I could tell Annie was worried that I was going to run. As if I wanted to be loose by myself out on one of these crummy country roads."

Dr. Gustafson came in then, sitting in the other armchair with his ever-present clipboard. It was time for our family therapy. I was actually looking forward to this because I knew that my parents—especially Dad—were very skeptical that anyone could teach them anything about being parents. My dad had called it "our so-called therapy session" on the phone last week when we were getting ready for their visit. My mother said, "Now, Ted," as if she partly agreed with him and partly thought they should go through with it because it was part of the program.

They were supposed to have read the first few chapters in some book about parenting. After some introductory baloney about the program, Dr. Gustafson said in his talking-down voice, "How did you find the parenting text?"

My dad stayed quiet, as he usually does at the beginning of any discussion when mom is in the room, and my mother said "It was very interesting."

In perfect shrink-talk, Gustafson asked "What was interesting about it?"

"Well, it didn't seem to say anything about children with special needs, such as bipolar or ADHD or autism or attachment or any of those challenges." My mother kept calling my brain's short circuits "challenges."

"And you see that as a problem?"

"I would assume that many of the girls here are coping with those kinds of challenges," my mother said. "So discussing parenting without any mention of mental illness and its impact on parent-child relations seems to leave out a lot—don't you think?"

Watch out, Mom—Gustafson asks the questions here.

"I understand why you might feel that is an omission," Gustafson said stiffly, without noticing how much the I understand slogan was pissing off my father. He looked down at his clipboard and made a few notes. I don't think Mom was getting any positive points.

Mom went on. "The other thing that struck me was that there was a lot of talk in the book about how important it is to be family-centered. We recognize that this session is part of that, but we only have the opportunity to have two or three of these in all the time Lexie is going to be here. I just wondered what it means when the book and your brochure talk about a 'family-centered program' if the family is not very involved in the program."

Wow, Mom, way to get in his face. I was starting to enjoy this. Gustafson was frowning more than I had ever seen him do in therapy. His whole deal was to never lose control by showing emotion. But he was showing emotion now, big-time.

And then my dad got into it. "Let me understand this. You cut off phone calls when the girls misbehave. So the family-centered approach means you block communications with the family whenever the girls have problems here? How does that make sense? And how is that family-centered?"

Then Gustafson really blew it.

"Mr. and Mrs. Crockett, I'm not sure you understand how family-centered we are. We've discussed your family quite a bit in our review of Lexie's progress."

My dad's body language is never very subtle. This time he almost jumped off the couch. "You *discuss* us?! And that's your definition of family-centered?"

And my mom started laughing—not a happy laugh—and said, "I can't believe you just said that!"

Gustafson did some double-talk about how he meant that they discussed my family but of course the staff also looked forward to interacting with us. Then Gustafson, trying to change the subject, asked me how I felt seeing my parents for the first time since I had gotten there.

"It's OK, but I'm still pissed at them for sending me away and taking over my life. They never want me to have control."

"And why do you think that is, Lexie?"

I was silent for a few moments, and then my dad spoke up before I could answer. "She's angry because we told her repeatedly that she would have to go to residential if she didn't obey our rules—and she just kept breaking our rules."

Gustafson said, with a kind of sneer, "Mr. Crockett, you're speaking for her. I had asked Lexie what she thinks." It was as though someone was keeping score, and Gustafson thought he'd won a point.

My dad answered, patiently, "No, I'm reminding her of what she's said before when we talked with her about all this. If you knew anything about her you'd know that sometimes her short-term memory needs a prompt. I respect what she says, and I show her I am listening when I remind her of what she has said."

The session went downhill pretty fast after that. My dad just sat and glared at Gustafson, and my mom kept talking about how much they wanted to be involved, and Gustafson kept saying that he understood—which made my dad even madder. I talked a little about how much my parents bugged me with all their rules. And then we ran out of time, which always seemed to happen whenever a therapy session got to something important.

Afterward, as my parents walked with me out to their rental car to head back to the airport, my mother looked at me and said, quieter than she usually talks to me, "Lexie, you talked in there about how you have no control here and no control at home. But you need to think about what that means. Because you're the only one with the power to turn this around. It really is in your control. You want control—you have it. Now use it to get your life out of the ditch where you've driven it. No one else can do it. You've got to work with this program so you can get home."

They hugged me, but didn't say much else and then they drove away.

I guess it wasn't just Gustafson they were pissed off at.

Later that day I was in therapy with Annie, in her office, feeling bummed about how the visit with my parents had gone. Annie asked me about it and I said I didn't want to talk about it—which of course made Annie ask me why not.

"Because they don't get it and nobody here gets it, and I'm sick of talking about it to people who don't get it."

"Don't get what?"

"Don't get what I want and how much I hate this place!"

Annie leaned back in her chair and looked at me, hard. "Lexie, we need to make sure you're not just blaming everybody else for what's happening to you." She paused, watching me. Then she asked, "Why are you bored all the time, Lexie? You tell me you hate it here, but you say you're always bored at home and so you run away. Why?"

"Because there's never anything to do in our house."

Annie scowled at me and then started in on a list, talking fast without giving me a chance to answer. "No books? No movies? No TV? No arts or crafts? No community service projects in your neighborhood? No kids around to babysit? No computer? No Internet service? No software to write stories or journals or anything? None of that exists in or around your house, Lexie? Because if that's so, you're really a deprived kid and I feel sorry for you—all those things you don't have."

It was as angry and sarcastic as I'd ever seen Annie get, and in the back of my mind I knew it had something to do with her sister. It was like the time she had blown up at Dolores for saying she was going to drop out of school when she got home. I knew part of what she was saying without putting it into words was that I took all that stuff for granted. It made me mad—but it also made see through Annie's eyes all the stuff I obviously had in my house that her sister didn't have living on the street. And that a lot of the girls here didn't have at home, either.

Annie went over to the whiteboard in her office and drew four circles that overlapped. "See if this makes any sense to you, Lexie. If it doesn't," she picked up the eraser, "then I erase it and we start over. But give me a chance first."

She wrote labels on each of the circles: what the bipolar does, what the program does, what the parents do, what Lexie does. "These are the pieces, as I see it. It is not all about your brain and body—but that matters. It's not all about what we're trying to do here in the program, and it's not just about your parents. These things come together, but you're in the picture too," she pointed to the circle she had labeled what Lexie does, "and part of what happens is absolutely about you—about whether you get it—not whether the rest of us get it." She stopped and looked at me with a little smile. "Do you buy any of this?"

I was quiet, looking at the circles. It did make sense, sort of, and what I liked about it was that it didn't say—the way my parents sometimes did—that it was all up to me. But it still bugged me that Annie was saying that I blamed everyone else. My father had this stupid refrain that I had heard a thousand times: "You always blame everyone else and you never accept responsibility yourself." The program at The Houses had taught us that always and never statements were wrong, and that you should avoid them if you want to have good communications with other people.

After waiting quietly, seeing that I was struggling with something, Annie asked "What are you thinking, Lexie?"

"That it makes some sense. But if nothing much is happening here," I pointed to the program circle and the parents circle, "then nothing much is going to happen here," pointing to the Lexie circle.

"So everybody else has to change first? And then you do your part of it?"

"No, I'm not saying that." I stopped, and thought about how hard Annie was pushing me. I didn't like it much, but it made therapy a hell of a lot more interesting than when she just sat back and asked me how I was feeling. And then I started to think about all the work that I had to do and how long it would be before I could get home, and it all seemed so hopeless. "I just don't know if I can do it—and I just want to go home."

"I know you can do it, Lexie. It isn't all up to you, but you'll get out what you put into it. And we all want you to get home just as soon as you are ready."

"So how do we know when I'm ready?"

"When these things"—she pointed to the four circles "are coming together. And when this one—the Lexie one—is out in front." She looked at her watch. "Time for group."

As we walked over to the education building, I thought about the session. I was feeling pissed off, because it still seemed like a lot of work and I didn't know if I could do it.

Group therapy was not my favorite time. We had to do it once a week, and I never looked forward to it. Some of the girls were what they called "therapy hogs," which meant they just talked and talked about their own stuff or, even worse, what they thought about the rest of us. So you get some bitchy bigmouth who is all full of herself telling all the rest of us what we're doing wrong, and how we're "very hostile" to her and how we have "an attitude problem."

When it wasn't irritating, it was boring, and what it had to do with "getting well" was a mystery to me.

But we had to do it, and if you skipped or refused to participate, you got lots of negatives and lost privileges. So everyone showed up and you had to at least say something. At first, I figured it was just another part of the phony stuff that went on all the time, pretending to be part of a group you would never choose to hang out with if you weren't basically locked up with them.

You had to be careful, though. If you never talked about yourself, sooner or later somebody would say "why aren't we hearing about your problems, Lexie?" But then if you went on too long about your own stuff, somebody would pop up and say "Oh, listen to Lexie's pity party." I made that mistake just once, when Annie asked me at the first therapy meeting to talk about why I was there. I started talking about running away and my parents and problems I had at school, and then Laurie chimed in and started in on the pity party routine. So I shut up.

In group Sophia was the only one who never talked. They gave her negatives, but it didn't phase her. She just waited until the staff said "5000 points in negatives, Sophia," and all she'd say was "Bifud." I finally asked her what it meant and she gave me a mean-looking smile and said "Big fucking deal."

As we went into the family room for group, I saw one of Laila's haiku where she had left it in the downstairs hallway on the table where staff put their keys.

> *In group therapy*
> *We offer up you and me*
> *So we all can see.*

Laila had this long, shiny, black hair that everyone envied. She never did anything with it—it just hung down to the middle of her back. She had an accent, but she spoke better English than most of us. I think her accent embarrassed her, though. Maybe she wrote the poetry because she had no accent in her poems.

Once in group when Annie had really pushed her to talk, she said very quietly "I don't like to talk about what happened before I was adopted and then brought here. It was very bad in the orphanage, and the little I remember before that was much worse." She shuddered, and then she lowered her head and stopped talking. Annie let her off after that, and she spoke little, usually about something someone had said about the whole group, never about herself.

16

Annie

Annie called the therapy group to order. The girls were restless, moving around on the sofa and chairs scattered around the large room off the kitchen that was used for TV watching and for weekly therapy sessions.

"Tonight we're going to talk about one of your favorite topics." She waited for the inevitable reactions.

"Sex, drugs, and hard rock?"

"Guys?"

"Girls?" This from one of the bi's.

Annie decided they had let off enough steam. "No, we're going to talk about therapy." She waited for the groans to die down. "Why do we do therapy?"

"To torture us."

"To bore us to death."

Belinda stretched out to her full, amazing length, put her hands behind her head, and said in a sing-song voice "Because it teaches us how to live our lives as good little girls."

Annie smiled and said "Thank you for the sarcasm, one and all. We do therapy because it helps us uncover some of the stuff we keep hidden—even from ourselves. Stuff that got you here and keeps you here. And because sometimes all of us together are smarter than any one of us by herself."

Lexie had been silent, but now she looked straight at Annie and said, "I have never learned anything in therapy that I didn't know already. Why waste the time?"

Annie decided to give her some room to make her point. "What would you rather do with the time?"

The answers came back from all over the room. "Sleep." "Eat." "Get laid.""Get high."

Annie kept watching Lexie. "What would you rather do, Lexie?"

Lexie was silent for a while, and the others waited for her. They had learned that Lexie wasn't afraid to butt heads with the staff, even Annie, and some of them were hoping for a verbal fight.

"I'd rather fix this damned place so it really does some good."

"How?"

Lexie smiled, finally, and said, "First, I'd fire all the staff—except you." She waited, while Annie nodded, letting her go on. "Then, I'd hire some new people—some people like us—girls who have been through a place like this and know what it's all about."

Annie wondered what she was getting herself into, but she saw that all of them were quiet, waiting to see where Lexie was going. She decided to keep the ball rolling. "Then what?"

"Then I'd make the parents come here for therapy. They need help as much as we do."

"Yes!" came from several girls at once. "Word, girl!"

"What else?"

Lexie shrugged. "I don't know. I haven't been here as long as some of you—what would the rest of you do?"

Annie marveled at how easily Lexie had gotten the others into it. It was rare that any of the girls could step out of her own self-absorption long enough to open the session up to others. But Lexie had done it naturally, easily. And it was like a dam had burst. The answers came back so fast Annie couldn't keep track of who said what.

"Kill the stupid points and levels system."

"No—let us have a points system for *them*."

"Yeah!" came back from several girls. "At the end of the month we add it up and the staff with the fewest points have to do deep cleans."

"No—they have to fire the one with the lowest score!"

"Let us hire a shrink who knows something about people like us."

"Get real teachers instead of retread house staff."

"Get some decent food."

"Let us buy the freaking food from a budget. We'd eat better and still save money."

"Let us watch real TV—if we earned it."

"Let the ones who earned it watch TV and stick the others in their rooms."

"Let us all bring our IPods from home."

"Let us wear our own clothes instead of these stupid sweat shirts that say The Houses. Sounds like we're a construction firm."

"*Ice cream.*"

The last one was so distant as a possibility that it silenced all of them for a moment. Laurie repeated it softly, as though she were saying holy words. "Ice cream."

Annie let the silence last for a while, thinking about all they had said and how quickly the ideas had tumbled out of them. Finally, she said, "Some pretty interesting ideas there." She turned back to Lexie. "You started something, Lexie."

Lexie sat smiling, pleased that she had been the center of something good for a change. Then she looked serious, and said to Annie, "Has there ever been a program like that—where the girls got to sort of run it by themselves?"

Dolores answered before Annie could. "Hell, no. They'd never trust girls like us. They'd be worried we'd screw it up for them. All their big jobs and all that. Who'd trust us?"

Annie said, "I don't know. Seems to me you earn trust. Nobody gives it to you—you earn it." She looked around at them, realizing she couldn't remember a time in therapy when the whole group had been this tuned in, listening and caring about the conversation. Like any good therapist, Annie knew that the silences were as important as the talking. She waited for the conversation to pick up again.

Belinda said, "What would it take to convince them to let us try it? Would they ever let us try it for some parts of the program—not the whole thing, but parts of it? Let us make some of the decisions, I mean."

Cautiously Annie said, "I don't know. But if all of you got together and agreed on some of these changes—not making the staff do deep cleans," she smiled, "but some of the other things—maybe they'd listen. Why don't you all talk about it among yourselves and see what you think?"

She watched their faces. A few of them looked skeptical and bored again, and started talking about what TV program they were going to choose. But she could see that Belinda and Lexie had given each other looks, and she wondered if anything would really happen.

Email
From: Annie Salinas to Geraldine Salinas
Subject: Listening to the girls

We had the greatest therapy session this week. I mostly shut up (for a change, I hear you saying!) and let the girls talk. And they poured out more ideas for improving our program than I've heard in years of staff meetings. I have no idea what is going to happen with their ideas, but it was a great reminder of how much can happen when you stop talking at "the clients" and just listen. It made me wonder how much I've missed working here and assuming that these girls have so many problems that they can't come up with solutions. We may not have hit on any real solutions, but they sure came up with some better ways of running the program. Imagine a 15-year-old girl saying they should switch the point system so that the staff was being graded instead of the girls!

Now I have to figure out how to keep the girls from feeling that we ignored them—and how to keep the staff from feeling that I've created a monster.

Stuck in the middle, as usual. But you know me—always pushing the edge.

Love you,
Annie

17

Lexie

JULY

Then it got hot. It got really hot, not like in Southern California where a few weeks in August and early September were sometimes air conditioner time. This heat went on and on, and it reminded us that we were living in a real desert, far away from the beach where any normal human being would spend as much of the summer as she could.

We went off to a national park for a week of camping. I hated camping. My idea of camping was renting the world's largest RV and sitting in it all day, going for a swim in a lake somewhere and watching TV and texting friends the rest of the time.

But this was real camping, in a tent with girls from the other houses. They mixed us up so we could "get to know some of the other residents." Just when I was getting to know the girls in Prospect, they throw us in with these other girls who were rich-bitch snobs or gangbanger wannabes. And three of us were in a tent together all night, with snoring and dumb stories about "back home" and some of the worst smells I have ever smelt anywhere. I hated it.

When we got back to Prospect, I felt like I was back to semi-normal. Maybe that was the idea—they tricked us into liking the house we were in by sticking us in a much worse place. It sort of worked for me.

In summer, everyone wore the same outfit, shorts but not very short and t-shirts, not very tight. We didn't wear a lot of high-end clothes, like at a high school where you could tell who was able to buy whatever clothes she wanted. But you could still see someone with a fancy new undershirt or some boots or a snow jacket that was definitely a cut above what most of the girls could afford.

The differences between the public girls and the private girls were never talked about by the staff, but we all knew pretty much who was who. It was tricky, because it wasn't just about who paid for you to be there. Some of the girls from not-terrible homes—like mine, I guess—were still paid for by school districts and county mental health agencies. But others were sent there by probation agencies, and they were usually girls with a lot more problems—or, as one of them said in therapy one time—with much worse lawyers than the rest of us could hire.

But even with these differences, one of the things I learned at Prospect was that some of the meanest girls could be from the richest families, and some of the nicest could be from the opposite end. I sort of wondered about that in school in Orange, but here it was obvious—a bitch was a bitch, whether she had on fancy boots or Wal-Mart knockdowns. And a girl who tried to help you could be from a family with a ton of money, or from almost no family at all.

One of the dumbest things we ever did turned out to be kind of helpful. This guy from the headquarters office came and got us into the family room and told us to sit wherever we would be most comfortable. Then he told us to pick a part of our body to focus on, or just pay attention to our breathing. Really focus on it, he said, not just think about it a little bit.

We rolled our eyes, but then we watched Laila, who had closed her eyes and was humming softly to herself. She was sitting kind of weird, with her legs crossed and her feet folded up into her lap. And she was smiling, more than we usually saw her smile. So we tried it. There was some giggling at first, and then it got quiet. And I actually felt relaxed, really relaxed, like I was ready for a nap but not tired, just ready to let all the stress go for a little while.

After a while, the guy told us that was enough and then explained it to us. He said if you're focusing, you can't mad or nervous because your brain is so full of whatever you're focusing on. I guess the idea is that your brain gets a rest when you're focused on one thing, instead of jumping around all the time. He talked about the way that TV and video games and cellphones make you more anxious with messaging and rings and new stuff flooding in all the time.

After he was gone, Laurie told us that her dad, who was in the military somewhere, had told her that they were training soldiers and pilots with this focusing technique, so they could keep track of targets and where the bad guys were when a whole lot of information was pouring in from satellites and spy cameras and audio stuff.

Funny—using focus to figure out who to kill. Here I guess they're trying to use it to figure out how to save our lives.

18

Annie

The summer months seemed to drag by, slow and hot. The only break the girls got from the heat was a week-long camping trip they took up into the mountains, which was a combination of wilderness school and conservation education. Annie tried to lighten the girls' load in the summer, knowing it was a hard time.

On the weekends, they took the van over to a local pool, where the girls were in constant trouble for the brevity of their bathing suits and the great interest in those suits on the part of the local male population. The staff spent hours going over the guidelines for bathing suits and taking the girls back to the local Wal-Mart to exchange too-skimpy attempts to ignore the guidelines. One of the girls from the other houses who could sew launched a very profitable underground enterprise, cutting down what the girls called the "granny" versions of the allowable suits and converting them to racier, more revealing outfits.

But during the week, with classes and therapy, fixing meals and clean-ups, the summer was mostly a reminder of how far they were from home. They knew that back home, only the nerds were in summer school. The girls from California endured nightly dreams of beach breezes and endless waves, from which they woke up hot and irritable.

Annie spent the summer months using a week of her vacation time at Balboa with a friend who had rented a house just off the sand on Oceanfront, and attending classes at the state university to brush up on therapeutic innovations. She also did some work with a counselor from one of the other houses who was training some of the junior therapists.

In one session, the counselor, named Teresa Johanssen, talked about the range of parents in the program. She told Annie and the rest of the team that in any group of ten parents, the group will divide roughly in half. The first half will be trying to do the right thing, and the second half either doesn't try or has no clue how to try. She said it was "the sixth parent" they were trying to get to—the one in the second group that might get it if the staff did a good job of working with them to turn things around.

Annie said "You mean we're aiming at the 'prodigal parent?'"

Teresa laughed and said "You could say that." She added, "There's no book or parenting program that will work for all of them. So what we have to do is figure out which ones might listen and what would help them hear something new. Some of them can't handle any kind of feedback at all. They're really in denial that they have anything to do with their daughter's problems. And some of them use our flaws—and we've always got some—as an excuse to keep theirs off the table.

"In one-on-one therapy with parents, you'll find it's usually easier to be quiet and let them complain—about their kid, about the program, about how hard it all is on them. But if you're that quiet, and they're doing most of the talking—there may not be much therapy going on. Just sitting there saying "OK, OK, I understand" over and over isn't therapy. And eventually even the most self-absorbed parents will catch on that you're not adding anything to the process.

"So ask them what questions they have. Ask them to do homework about other programs and about parenting. Shift from questions about us to questions about them. They'll resist—but it's your job."

Annie had an apartment in a new building about five miles from The Houses, in a small town containing several churches, a gun store, a mini-Wal-Mart, and a dirt racing track. The town had little to recommend it—which is why Annie liked it.

She had spent a lot of time fixing up her apartment as a kind of retreat from the intensity of the work with the girls and the rest of the staff. She had made wall shelves for several pieces of antique pottery her grandfather had given her from the collection he brought from Vera Cruz. And she had carefully framed pictures of Vera Cruz that she had taken on a trip with her sisters to the Mexican Gulf Coast three years ago.

Annie wasn't much of a cook, so her kitchen was nondescript. But she loved beer, and her refrigerator was almost entirely filled with her collection of every known Mexican beer and a few more from other parts of Central and South America.

After the training at the central office, Annie had introduced herself to Greg Wisnewski. They had only talked for a few minutes, because there were several other people from the other sites who wanted to talk with him. But something had happened, because the next day she got an email from him asking if he could meet with her the next time he was out at The Houses. Annie quickly said yes.

They had met for lunch once, and Annie found herself warming to the tall researcher. He was easy to talk to, though a little shy, and Annie found herself enjoying having most of the control over the conversation, which stayed very light and non-serious. She was getting ready to graduate to dinner, and wondered if Greg was going to make a move. Then she decided to make the move first. So she invited him to a Chinese restaurant close to The Houses for dinner.

They ordered, and Annie began the conversation by asking "So how did you get into this work?"

Greg explained that he had gotten his PhD in educational research at UCLA, but the first full-time job he found was with the parent company for The Houses in Desert City. He loved to ski, and being that close to a dozen resorts was irresistible. Then he started learning more and more about the girls who were in residential treatment, and the work became much more than a job. As he talked, he looked at Annie, and then glanced away, not smiling much, in a way that made

Annie feel he was being cautious, withholding something from the conversation. Whenever the conversation touched on his job and his superiors, he became cautious and vague. Annie remembered him standing up to Suzanne in his first presentation and she wondered if that was his style—or just a temporary break from his usual caution.

Greg asked the appropriate questions about Annie's job history, and she told him the broad outlines of how she got to The Houses. She touched lightly on her sister's history, and ended up her spiel saying "So it's much more than a job for me, too. But it looks like it's about to change with the new owners. And I don't know what to do about it."

Greg said, "Me neither. But how about we have dinner again next week and keep talking about it?"

Surprised, Annie agreed, and they made it a date.

As Annie drove home, she replayed the conversation and found herself looking forward to the next dinner. Greg was smart, and he understood her work, which made it easy to go back and forth between talking about themselves and the work. But she wasn't sure that she really knew who he was yet. She decided to keep trying to find out.

19

Lexie

When I first got here, I thought one of the dumbest things was these little sayings they made us learn. They were supposed to help us to have "useful conversations," according to Gustafson. One of the ones I got sick of real fast was this thing you were supposed to say when you wanted to have a difficult conversation: "Do you have a minute?" And then you were supposed to say what you thought the person you were talking to was thinking, so you could show that you were thinking about them instead of just yourself.

So it went like this:

"Annie, do you have a minute? I understand that you may think that I haven't earned being able to go to get pizza tonight because of what happened in class today, but I have really been trying to get along with everybody, etc. etc."

At first it all seemed like a bunch of crap. But then I found myself using it with my parents on the phone. And it really did sort of help make the conversation easier, because I guess they heard me trying to listen to them for a change and not be disrespectful. I used to get so mad at them I didn't care what I said. The old way, I'd ask them for something, they'd say no, then I'd start yelling "your rules suck" or "you never let me do anything!" or "I hate you."

But this way, I had to think about where they were coming from. I realized I didn't do that very much—I just assumed that they were going to say no and I never thought about how to make my case carefully.

I never focused on what they cared about, but just demanded what I wanted and then got mad right away when I didn't get it.

My dad made me so mad sometimes when we started into one of these battles. He had this stock response that I hated. When I told them something I wanted to do or wanted them to buy for me, he would ask me if I remembered "the words of the great British philosopher, Mick Jagger," and then he would start singing, totally off-key, "You don't always get what you want."

It always cracked him up, and it always pissed me off.

Then in summer school, we had a debate in our American Government class. The teacher appointed me head of my team, and we began to prepare our arguments. The topic was the three strikes law about locking people up after three felonies. And I wrote out some pretty good arguments and worked really hard with my team, even though some of the girls didn't care about it and wouldn't do any of the prep work.

When the day of the debate came, I was really nervous. I knew all the stuff we had prepared, but I was still worried about whether I would be able to think on my feet when I heard the arguments from the other side. We went first, and then they went, and then it was our turn for rebuttal. And as I started talking, standing at this fancy lectern, I got this funny feeling like I do sometimes when I am running and I get into a groove and everything comes easy.

I had made notes on their arguments, and one by one, I demolished them, because I remembered all the stuff we had prepared for counter-arguments. While I was talking, I could see some of the girls sitting with their mouths open, surprised at how well I was doing. The girls on my team made quiet little clapping motions with their hands.

At the end, we lost. But I almost didn't care, because I knew I had done well. I had tried something hard and it didn't defeat me. That felt fantastic. And when the teacher finally gave out the grades—I got the highest grade in the class!

It was the neatest thing—I got to argue—and everybody clapped for me! Sometimes, it turns out, arguing is the right thing to do. If you do it right.

The teacher in the class that held the debate was a woman who had worked in the federal government. Her name was Dianne Dozier, and she told us she had worked in the U.S. Department of Education in Washington. A few days after the debate she said she wanted to see me after class.

I was pretty nervous when I walked in to her classroom. She asked me to sit down and said "Lexie, I wanted to make sure you knew how good a job you did in the debate, and what it might mean to your future."

"My future?"

"Yes." She smiled. She was very pretty, with short blonde hair. I looked up at a picture of her on the wall behind her desk. It was Dianne standing with the President. "That's from when I was a Presidential intern ten years ago."

"Wow."

"Yes—that was a good day. But I get as much enjoyment from seeing you girls do well in my classes here. And I really liked seeing how good you were the other day. You took the arguments you had prepared, and you made your case, and when the other team disagreed, you took their arguments and answered every one of them. You were very good, Lexie. You really deserved that A." She stopped and looked at me. "Do you know what Lex means—what your name means?"

"Sure—it's short for Alexandra."

"Yes, of course. But Lex in Latin means the law. Have you ever thought about being a lawyer?"

When she said it, a light seemed to go on in my head. "A lawyer? Me?" I giggled. "My mom and I used to watch *Law and Order* together all the time. I even memorized the whole Miranda warning. But be a lawyer?"

"Yes. A lawyer takes the arguments for or against a case and puts them together to try to convince a judge or a jury. You could do that. You could represent people who need help—even people like these girls."

It was the first time in my life anybody had said I was good at something and then tried to connect it with work I could do. It was hard for me to think about. But it felt really good to have her care enough to make the suggestion, and to believe that I could do it.

"Thanks. Can I think about it some more and maybe come talk to you about it?"

"Definitely. You make sure you do that, Lexie."

I had tried to talk to Sophia several times since she'd arrived. But each time she just mumbled a few words and didn't seem to want to make any effort at all. So I left her alone.

But one afternoon she was walking by herself, headed back to Prospect from the classroom building. So I caught up to her and walked beside her. Then I asked her "How's it going?"

She looked at me, seeming surprised that I had spoken to her. Then she put back on her pissed-off mask and said "It sucks."

"Yeah, I know. I hated it when I first got here. I still do, but you get used to some of it." I decided whatever she said I was not going to give up trying to make contact with her.

"I'm never going to get used to it," she said. "I'm getting out of this dump as soon as I can get my boyfriend to come and get me."

"You talk to him?" We were not allowed to talk to anyone not on the "approved by family" list.

"Yeah. He fixed up his phone so it looks like my parents' number. He's some kind of electronic genius and he can do stuff like that."

"How are you going to get out?"

She walked along for a while, not answering, and then she shrugged. "I've been kicked out of two places before this. It's easy—you just threaten them, hit a staff member once or twice, kick a few holes in the wall. Pretty soon they give up. They're glad to get rid of you. They can't throw you in isolation forever—takes too much staff time."

I couldn't figure out her thought process. "Yeah, but then they send you to a lock-down program."

"If you act crazy enough, you can get kicked out of any program." Then she stopped walking and pointed her finger at me, scowling. "I know you're trying to be nice, but I don't need it. I'm pretty much a loner, and I like it that way. OK?"

"Sure—whatever." We walked back to the house together, but neither of us said anything more. I'd tried, and she just wasn't into talking to anyone.

I wondered if Annie could get through to her.

And then, a few nights later, Sophia finally opened up a little, one night while the rest of the girls were watching TV. She was sitting alone in the living room where Evelyn could still see her but not hear anything. I went over and sat down, and she just started talking to me. As she talked, she kept picking at an old pillow that had been on the couch.

Sophia told me she'd seen Annie a lot during the past week. Annie had doubled up her therapy sessions—staff could do that when they thought you needed extra attention. Annie had seen Sophia every day for a week, and Sophia admitted it had really helped her to finally have someone to talk to.

"Annie's really different. Don't get me wrong—I hate this place and I'm getting out as soon as i can. But Annie makes it a little easier to be here. She really listens to me. She knows when I'm BSing her, and she calls me on it right away."

I agreed, "Got that right. She nails you."

"Yeah. She let me rant and rave the first time I saw her, and then at the end she just said, 'Sophia, what can I do for you? How can we work together to get you home?' It was so calming to hear that, Lexie. She seems like a really peaceful, laid-back chick, you know?"

I liked Annie a lot, and I could tell that Sophia had really connected with her. Then she said, lowering her voice and looking toward Evelyn and the girls at the other end of the room "Annie said I could talk to you."

That blew me away. It made me feel that somehow Annie had given me a recommendation, one that I needed to try to live up to now. So I said I'd be glad to listen, and Sophia started talking.

At the end, I almost wished she hadn't told me her story. It was like all of our stories—but a lot worse. She lived with her aunt—her parents had broken up and her mother was in prison. Her aunt was into drugs and Sophia knew it was a bad place for her. The boyfriend who was going to come and get her never got mentioned again, and I didn't want to bring it up. She said she might be able to live with a friend when she went home, but it sounded pretty vague to me.

"So how did you get here, anyway?" I asked her.

"The school district reported me to Probation when I kept cutting school, and Probation made county mental health and the school district pay for me to come here after I got kicked out of the last place." She wouldn't look at me, but her voice was so sad. "I hate it here, but at least I'm safe. If I go back there, I'm afraid one of my aunts' scumbag boyfriends will . . ." She didn't finish it, but she didn't need to.

I still couldn't figure her out. When I talked to her before, she'd wanted to get out and go home. Now, it seemed like home was no better than being here. What a crummy deal—hating it here and hating it at home just as much.

"You know," Sophia said, "this place isn't as bad as some." She started talking about the places she had been before, mostly about the last place. She called it "the hellhole," and I think that was partly because she hated saying the name of the place so much.

Once she started talking, I knew she needed to keep going and I just tried to listen as quietly as I could. She was so intense I worried a little that she would start yelling, but she just kept on telling me what she had been through, going into more detail than I had ever heard her talk about, in group or anywhere else. And she kept picking at the pillow, pulling off the edging and digging at the insides.

"It was a terrible place, Lexie. I hated every minute I was there, and all I could think about was how to get out, how to run away or get kicked out."

"Sounds different from here."

"Here? Here, sometimes you can relax. There—never. You always had to be watching your back to make sure that staff or other girls weren't planning some way of messing you up. It was all about survival in that place. I was constantly watching over my shoulder to see who was going to jump me or somebody next to me. I've read about prisons, where everybody gets into gangs or some kind of protection group. This was like that. If you were out on your own, you were dead meat. There was a fight almost every day. I got jumped on four times in the first month I was there."

She looked around, and made a face like she'd smelled something bad. "Don't get me wrong—I don't want to be here, either, but this is like heaven compared to that hellhole."

She kept talking, fast, waving her arms, like she needed to tell someone how bad it was. "The building we were in was like somebody tried to combine a hospital with a penitentiary. There were 240 girls there, 20 to a wing in a three-story building. Each floor had four wings. Nobody had painted it in a long time and there was paint coming off the inside and outside. It fell off in big flakes, all the time. Big cobwebs up on the ceiling in all the corners.

She went on. "The staff was awful. They must have been recruited at a convention of wannabe prison guards."

"Where'd all the good people go, huh?"

She shook her head and looked really sad. "There were no good people there, Lexie. None."

She was quiet and then kept talking. "There was a sick thing going on there between the dykes on the staff and the 'gay for the stay' girls. I have some really close friends back home who were real lesbians, and

I had worked out how to be around them without getting into the girlfriend stuff. I liked them because they were so honest about their lives—not just the sex stuff, but their whole lives. They had learned to be honest about who they were, and I respected that. But in the hellhole, it was sick. The staff and a girl would disappear into the supervisor's office for what they called a disciplinary session, and we'd hear lots of giggling, and it would get quiet, and then the girl would come out of the office all messed up, fixing her clothes."

"Hard to imagine that happening here without someone finding out."

"That was the thing, there was this culture there of no one tells, and it got to be a way of keeping all these secrets about some really abusive stuff that was happening to some of the girls.

"I spent a lot of time in what they called the CDR—calm down room. They'd throw you in there for anything—not like here where you only go to isolation if you really flip out. There, you'd get sent to CDR for arguing with staff, for swearing at another girl—anything they didn't like. If you didn't get up on time, they'd grab your mattress and throw you on the floor. They didn't touch you, so they could say they weren't rough with the girls. But they would flip you through the air inside your mattress, and you could fall out and hit something on the floor. One girl got a concussion. And the therapy was a joke. For three weeks, they just let us watch *Prison Break* on TV and called it therapy group."

"You just watched TV?!"

"Yeah. It made it easier for the staff, and there weren't enough therapists to go around. You were supposed to see your therapist once a week in one-on-ones, but it was usually for 15 minutes—sometimes it was in the hall because they were so busy. They'd tell us if we had any problems to write a note that you wanted to see the therapist on a special yellow slip that they gave us. Then we were supposed to slip the note under the door of the therapist if you wanted to see one of them." She laughed. "One time I was in the therapist's office and she opened her bottom desk drawer to get something and I saw piles and piles of yellow slips in there. I sent those notes twice and then gave up. I figured it was just to make us think something would happen and quiet us down when we had complaints about the staff.

"They never let us go outside—never. We had an inner courtyard and we could walk around in there—and that was it. In the summer, they took five of us at a time to a lake nearby and we could paddle around for a few hours and then get back in the van and go back to the facility."

"And I thought this place was bad."

"There are a lot of places like this, Lexie. Hundreds of them, with thousands of girls like us in them. Some are not bad—and some are really terrible, like the hellhole. Some are so bad they make girls worse than they were when they got there." She stopped and looked around. Three of the girls from our house were in the kitchen getting ready for dinner. Staff were nowhere in sight. She went on. "All these places have some bad staff—like Kendra here. But at the hellhole, there were no good staff at all.

"I've known girls who'd run away from home a few times and had used drugs or gotten drunk two or three times—and got sent to one of these places because their parents and their schools couldn't handle them. Not badass lawbreakers, you know, just kids who were having a hard time at home. And after they went through one of the bad places, they turned out so mean they could never get themselves in control again. Staff and the people who run places like that have this warped idea that if you punish a girl over and over, she'll finally shape up. And some girls do—they cave in and go along with the program and do whatever it takes, whatever fake stuff they need to do so they can get out of there.

"But other girls—if the punishment is really unfair—if they give out negatives and throw you in isolation for little things, then you know you're not in control. Some girls just give up trying." She was talking even faster now, getting angrier as she told me about the bad programs.

"And in a bad place, that means the program is just making the girls harder and meaner. And when they finally do get out, they can't go back to being OK. I knew two girls like that in our school. They went away to RTCs and came back and were kicked out of school right away and just sat around and smoked weed and waited until they turned 18 when everyone could forget about them for good."

"How did you stand it?"

She smiled, a sort of *I'm a lot smarter than you think* smile. "The same way I'm going to get out of here—I figure out what will get me kicked out and I wait for a chance to do it."

I was a little weirded out by how casually she talked about breaking the rules—big rules, not the little day-to-day ones. I decided to risk asking her a tough question—one I don't even like to think about myself. "Sophia—where do you think you'll end up?"

She looked at me, all the tough guy stuff gone now, with the saddest face I had seen in a long time. She tossed the pillow back on the couch, and shrugged. "I don't know. Dead or locked up, I guess."

20

Annie

Annie had thought a lot about Greg's lecture on the results of treatment, and she had an idea of what she could do about it. She was in the office one afternoon after therapy sessions were over, and had just ended a phone call when Suzanne walked in.

Suzanne looked very disturbed. "Annie, what are you doing? Central office said you asked for a list of all the girls who have been at Prospect for the past five years. Are you going to try to get in touch with them?"

Annie quickly answered, "That's exactly what I'm doing. Wouldn't you think we'd want to see how those girls are doing—to see if the program helped them? But when I checked, I found out that we have no effort at all under way to follow up on the outcomes of our program. Greg was talking about us when he talked about programs that don't follow up."

Suzanne switched to her *you don't understand* tone. "Annie, you know we can't be responsible for everything that happens to those girls after they get home. Some of them have hopeless parents, and none of that changes while they're here. The parents that need the most help refuse to even participate in our parenting programs. So how can you blame us for what happens to them after they leave here?"

Annie said, "I'm not blaming us—I just want to see how our graduates are doing." She looked down at a spreadsheet she had printed out. "So far, of the ones I can find, only a little less than half are stable. The others are in prison, had kids and lost them to child protective services, are unemployed, living in shelters, or we just can't find them at all—which may mean they're on the streets."

"Annie, I know you're very sensitive to girls who have problems because of . . ." Suzanne looked for a careful phrase, "your own family situation. But you need to be very careful with these results. What you're doing isn't scientific, and it may be violating the privacy of girls who were here. And it's not a good time to be questioning what we're doing, with the ownership changes under review."

"I'm not going to publish any of this," Annie said with a frown. "And I'm certainly not using any names. I just want to find out more than the tiny bits of information we now collect about what happens to these girls." Wanting to placate Suzanne and get back to her work, she added, "Look, I'll finish this round of calls and write up the results. Then I'll only show them to you—they won't go anywhere else. And then you can decide what we should do with them. OK?"

Suzanne agreed, reluctantly. But Annie knew that the results she was pulling together were real dynamite. She had actually finished the last of her calls, and the results were not very positive. She decided to talk with Greg about it the next time she saw him.

Annie was sitting in on an English class, as she sometimes did to check how girls were doing in their academics. The class was studying musicals as an American art form, and they had picked *West Side Story*. Annie wondered if the half-century old, cleaned up, Broadway version of gang life was the attraction, the eternal sweetness of the Romeo and Juliet story—or just Bernstein's classic music. Whatever it was, most of the girls were unusually quiet, which was not customary when a movie was shown in class.

And then Natalie Wood began "singing" the words to Annie's favorite part of the musical, and the girls all hushed, and Annie's heart ached for just a moment, for them, for Irene, and for all the girls who wanted to be "Somewhere" where there was a place for them and someone who cared about them. The soaring melodic line which

Bernstein had borrowed so easily from Beethoven lay under the lyrics, a few girls hummed along softly, and Annie felt a rare moment of grace for herself and her girls.

And she remembered the mother, in the parents' session a few months back, talking about the song "Somewhere Out There" from the Fievel movie and how sad it made her feel. From Spielberg to Bernstein—Annie felt she was back in her American Studies class at Fullerton. But she had learned that art—both popular and higher-toned—could sometimes remind her what the lives of these girls were about. Girls who wanted to be somewhere—and knew they weren't.

The summer parents' meeting was usually not well-attended, because some of the girls were on home leave for family vacations. Suzanne had asked Annie to handle it by herself, and she was looking forward to it. Four sets of parents showed up, and they spent the first half hour or so asking questions about the program that seemed to Annie to be mostly about complaints from their daughters.

Finally one of them, Holly's adoptive mother asked, "How do you know when to push them and when to let them go? It seemed like when Holly was home we were always trying to balance everything, remembering all that attachment stuff they told us about, but also trying to show her how normal people treat each other and not letting her abuse us all the time when she loses her temper. How do you know when to push and when to let it go?"

Annie had decided by this time that she was going to wade in and try to help, given how hard some of the parents were trying to deal with the changes. So she spoke up.

"I need to say something, if I can, because I see what you are trying to do from this side. I am just in awe of how hard some of you keep trying. I hear the abuse some of these girls give you on the phone when you call, and they want to go home, and they get so abusive with you to try to make you come and get them. I hear that, and sometimes when we are on speakerphone, I also hear how hard you are trying to keep under control despite all the abuse.

"We had some parents here a few years ago, and I'll never forget a story they shared with us. Their daughter was dually diagnosed, coping with mental illness and drug problems. And so they went to Al-Anon to try to get some help living with an addict. And somebody else told them they should join NAMI—the National Association on Mental Illness, so they could understand families affected by mental illness. And so they kept going to both sets of meetings, week after week, until they finally realized that Al-Anon was telling them to let go and NAMI was saying hang on."

The nods around the room made Annie feel her story wasn't completely off the point, and she continued.

"When I hear you talking, I know that we here will never face the same obstacles you deal with at home. But we're both struggling with figuring out when to hold back and when to come down on them and hold them accountable. Sometimes we go too far and punish them for acting out, forgetting the disorders and the damage. And sometimes we cut them too much slack, and don't push them hard enough to behave responsibly. But we hope we can continue to talk to you about where those lines are, and how we're drawing them and how you will be able to do it at home." And Annie went on to talk about specific incidents they had gone through lately, not using any of the girls' names, but showing the parents where they had tried to reinforce good behavior, and where they had, in fact, sometimes drawn the line.

And Annie heard one mother say to another under her breath as they left the room, "Wish they were all like her." And she felt good, for a few moments, and then she felt bad, because she knew it was more a statement about the rest of the program than about her.

21

Lexie

Belinda and I had spent some time after school in the library talking about the things we had all come up with in the therapy session when Annie let us talk about what was wrong with the program. It had been exciting, in a way, and neither of us wanted to let it just fade away. We weren't sure how to make it real, but we agreed that we would try and see what happens. After listening to Sophia talk about a really bad program, I kind of felt like we should try to do whatever we could to make ours better, as long as Annie was encouraging us.

Annie had agreed that she would let us combine our own weekly therapy sessions and talk with her about the changes we had proposed and then try to decide which of them were ideas that we could take to Suzanne. Annie warned us that there was no guarantee that any of it would be taken seriously, and I could tell that she was a little nervous herself about getting in trouble for encouraging us to come up with changes. But she told us that she believed in girls having more of a say in their programs, and she was willing to give it a shot.

She used the whiteboard in her office, and we gradually filled it up with ideas for change. It went fast when it was just the three of us. Belinda had a very realistic way of thinking about the program, and she could see which ideas were going to be too threatening and which we might be able to get through the staff and their supervisors. And my contribution was to think of how we could make our case for the changes. Belinda would take an idea and talk about how it would really work. And then I would throw out arguments we could use to convince Suzanne—first her arguments against it, then our counters to persuade her. We got into a real flow—Belinda tossing out an idea, me adding the best way to sell it, and Annie writing it all down.

It was one of the best therapy sessions we ever had, because it wasn't therapy that was trying to fix us. For a change, we were trying to fix the program.

We kept coming back to the points and levels system, because that was what bothered us the most, Annie had given us a copy of an article she had found in a psychology journal about what was wrong with points systems. It turns out some other residential programs had already developed alternatives to the points and levels stuff. They called it "problem-solving approaches," with a team from the facility talking through different ways of doing what points and levels tries to do. So we decided that we were going to ask if a committee of girls and staff could use the article to open up a discussion about changing the point system.

When we were done, I felt like we had run a marathon. But it felt great. Even if the staff didn't agree with any of the ideas, we had taken our best shot at changing the program, instead of just sitting around complaining. Now we'd see if anybody agreed with us.

When we went back to the house, I went upstairs to my room. Amanda was putting up some new pictures on her bulletin board, pictures of friends and movie stars.

Each girl was allowed to put up pictures and a few personal things to "decorate" her room. But staff were basically clueless about what things meant, and it got to be a game among the druggies to put up stuff that had a hidden drug theme. One of the girls had a marijuana leaf up for months, telling the staff it was a maple leaf because her mother was from Canada. Then Annie went upstairs one day and saw it and made her take it down. Another girl had a poster of Kurt Cobain who died of a heroin overdose. But no one on staff had a clue about who he was.

Some of the things the girls put up were just sad. Dolores had a picture of her dog, which she said her parents got rid of when she was sent away to The Houses, because there was no one to take care of it. Laurie had a picture of her little sister, who looked about 5 and was waving and holding up a sign saying "Laurie, I miss you." And Belinda had a picture of her horse back in Kentucky, in a big field bordered by tall white fences.

I had put up a picture of my family and a picture of me skiing at June Mountain.

Sophia had absolutely nothing on her walls.

Part Two

22

Annie

OCTOBER

Annie's monthly meeting with Suzanne Ellison was usually scheduled at the central office, but Suzanne had called and said she was going to be at The Houses and would be able to meet with Annie there. Suzanne usually came out only for parents' meetings and for a quarterly program review, so Annie wondered what had brought her out to the site.

Suzanne had set up her temporary office in Mountain House, which was at the head of the cul-de-sac. Deborah Wong was just walking out of the office as Annie came in. Deborah had a frown on her face and when Annie spoke to her, she simply said "Annie" as if acknowledging her was all she was able to do at that point.

Annie sat down in a chair opposite the desk where Suzanne had spread out her files. Suzanne said "Hello, Annie." She sat for a moment and looked at some papers in front of her, which Annie read as an attempt to cool off from whatever confrontation she had just had with Deborah. "You've been with us how long now—four years?"

"Five years last month."

"Five years. And you've received promotions and pay raises, and become one of the support therapists in your house."

"Yes." Annie had no idea where this was going, but she knew something was going on. Her meetings with Suzanne were usually routine, with Suzanne bringing Annie up to date on staff changes and procedures and then inviting her to ask any questions that she had. Annie usually obliged with one or two innocuous questions, and the session, which rarely lasted more than half an hour, was over. But this one seemed different to Annie from the outset.

"Annie, you've heard all the talk about our possibly being acquired by a new owner." Annie nodded. "Those negotiations are going well, and it looks as if they will be final in a few weeks. As part of the negotiations, the new owners have begun telling us what changes they're considering."

Annie remembered that she had meant to ask Monica about her father's knowledge of the acquisition, but hadn't gotten around to it yet.

Suzanne went on. "The new owners have a somewhat different idea of staffing ratios, and may be changing a few other procedures as well." Annie could tell that Suzanne was trying very hard to explain the changes as if she agreed with them, but Annie knew her well enough to know it was a false front. Suzanne didn't agree with them—at all.

"What this means to you is that you may have to pick up some more responsibility. You would be compensated for the increase in your responsibilities. But we'd reduce staffing in each house by one person, and reduce the therapy sessions that you've been holding so you would have more time for a supervisory role."

The arithmetic was clear: Pay her $5,000 more and get rid of a $25,000 salary with fringes. But measured against ten girls who could be very difficult—it was a hell of a way to save money. And then she realized that cutting out the therapy sessions, after she had worked five years to be assigned that role, meant that she was really taking a professional step backward, whatever the pay increase.

Suzanne was still waiting for her reaction. Annie asked, "Are you sure that eliminating a full-time position is the right thing to do for the girls?"

For a moment Suzanne's mask fell, and Annie saw how deeply the change was affecting her. Suzanne slowly said. "I've spent a lot of time thinking about that, Annie. It's a very good question." She was silent for a long time, looking down at Annie's file, until Annie began to wonder if the meeting was over. Then Suzanne spoke again, under more control.

"I think we can make it work. With the help of the more experienced staff, people like you, we can make it work. I'm sure of it."

But Annie heard Suzanne's effort to convince herself as much as she was trying to convince Annie. And she wondered if either of them was buying it, and if it would matter if they didn't. And then she thought about the great therapy session she'd had, with the girls coming up with all their ideas about making the program better. She had mentioned briefly to Suzanne that the girls had some ideas for changes in the program, and Suzanne was non-committal. But Annie knew that none of that would happen if the new people had their way—whoever the new people really were.

Then Suzanne shook her head. "Annie, I feel like I have to warn you about what you're doing. This outcomes study, asking the girls to suggest program changes—these may cause some problems. At a time when the ownership is changing, it may not be the best time to try to change things or ask questions about how things are done here."

Annie looked away and said quietly, "Maybe that's the best time to make changes—so they can see how much different it all could be."

Suzanne was silent, and then smiled at Annie. "Annie, if all the staff here had your outlook, it would be a very different place."

Annie was having a hard time figuring Suzanne out. First she'd warned her about what she was doing, and then she complimented her. Or at least it seemed like a compliment. Annie began to wonder whether Suzanne might be a lot more complicated than she had thought. Maybe Suzanne agreed with her about the harm that could result from the staffing changes.

She said to Suzanne, "I'll think about your . . ." she paused, "your 'warning.' And your ideas about a change in my role."

Suzanne seemed to want to say more, but then waved it off and just said. "Fine, Annie. Get back to me before the end of the week."

Annie went back to her office, leaned back in her chair, and looked up at her wall. Her father smiled back at her, from a photo taken when he was standing out of front of his first restaurant, beaming with pride, his arms folded over his large chest. And Annie remembered one of her last conversations with him before she left to start the job at The Houses.

"Annie, one of the things I do best is something I know you'll be good at, too, because of who you are. And that is asking hard questions. In business, the guys who ask the hard questions aren't jerks—they're doing their job, and they're making people think harder than they want to. And sometimes—sometimes, baby, they ask hard questions because they care so much about trying to get the answers right. So ask hard questions, honey, OK?"

And she knew she had done that, and it felt like the right thing to do.

23

Lexie

I was sitting in science class, and looked up to see Sheila Moore, the girl Belinda had called "the hacker" sitting at the desktop computer at the side of the classroom. The teacher had assigned us some test review material, and I wondered why Sheila was working on the desktop.

Carefully, I walked back to the bookshelf in the back of the room to get a biology book. I came back to my desk by way of the desktop, and whispered to Sheila, "What's up?"

She gave me a sly look at said "Wanna see? Belinda said you were maybe interested."

We both looked up, but the teacher was busy writing something. She was fairly tolerant of talking in class if it wasn't disruptive.

Shelia hit a key and I saw that the screen she had been working on was just a cover. She had a website open—already violating every rule in the program—and when I looked closer, I saw that the name at the top of the page was the teacher's name—Karen Prentice. Sheila was looking at her bank account!

"Holy shit! How do you do that?" I whispered.

"That's easy. Watch this." She hit a few more keys and what came up was another bank account. I couldn't figure out whose it was until I noticed that it wasn't a person's—it was a company called "The Houses—a 501(c)3 Corporation." Then it hit me—she was looking at the accounts of the whole program for The Houses!

"Ohmigod! I can't believe you're doing that. You must be the best hacker in this state."

"Fourth best, probably. I talk to the others all the time." She frowned. "They put me down because I'm a girl."

The teacher glanced up, and then went back to her work. I whispered to Sheila, "Can we talk after class?"

"Sure. See you back at Prospect."

When we finally found a place out on the back porch where we could talk without anybody else hearing us, I took a good look at Sheila. She was short, wore glasses, and had a long ponytail. I remembered there had been some problem upstairs in one of the bathrooms about her hair clogging the sink or something. She was twirling her hair and seemed a little nervous.

"You're not going to tell anyone, are you?"

I said, "No way. You're a genius, and I wouldn't dream of messing with what you can do." Then I laughed. "But I might want to talk to you about how to use your magic tricks."

"Like what?"

I had been thinking about it ever since I had seen what she could do. "That last screen you showed me means we could figure out how this whole place works—how they spend money and what they spend it on." Then I realized that I had actually learned something from my accountant father somewhere along the line. I decided to think about that later.

"Sheila, why are you here—if you don't mind my asking? All I remember you talking about in group was some problem with your parents."

"Sort of. They didn't like my emptying their bank accounts." She had a funny little smile, and I could see that she was really very shy, and used her computer skills to reach out into a world that mostly ignored her.

"What did you do with the money?"

"They had a lot of it. More than they could use. So I sent some of it to Darfur and used some for women's shelters."

I was blown away. I was ready for some story about jewelry or drugs or some guy she met. But she was a modern-day Robin Hood, taking from the rich—with her parents at the top of the list.

She went on. "I never would have been caught if I hadn't taken their money. But they made me mad. They have all this stuff in a big house and never gave anything to charity. So I did it for them. Then the teacher at my school, who knows my mother, had me classified as Oppositional-Defiant. And the next time I did it, they reported me to the cops." She giggled. "You're the only one who ever asked me about it. Belinda just wanted to talk to her boyfriend on email."

She looked at me, still twisting her ponytail. "So what do you want me to do?"

I took a deep breath and began, trying not to say anything that would scare her away. "Here's what I'm thinking about—but I want to talk to you about it before we do anything, so you can help me figure out whether this even makes sense. You know how they give us all this cheap food and use old textbooks and stuff like that?"

She nodded. "Sure. Everybody assumes they're ripping somebody off. Old milk, old bread, Kool-Aid, generic toilet paper. The whole thing."

"What if we knew how much they got for each of us—from the parents who pay, from school districts and county and state agencies? And then we could see who they pay it out to—what they pay for food and utilities and other stuff. Then we'd know how much profit they make."

"Then what?"

Once again, I remembered a lecture from my father about how I never think about what happens if I break a rule or a law—he called it "what's next" thinking. Sheila was a "what's next" thinker, which turns out to be a pretty rare thing. And a good thing.

I went on, not at all clear where I was going. "I'm not sure. Then maybe we go to them and say we want better stuff because we know they could afford it."

"But then they'd know that we hacked them." She had the worried look back on her face.

"Oh. Right. Well, that's why we have to think this through."

She seemed reassured. "Let me see what I can get for you, and maybe it will help us figure out what the next step is."

"Great."

And so the Great Profit Analysis Hacking Caper began.

If I'd known where it was going to end up, I never would have started. Talk about not figuring out the next step.

24

Annie

Annie had been thinking a lot about her conversation with Suzanne, and was getting more and more upset about Suzanne's reaction. So she called Greg and said she wanted to talk with him about her work on outcomes. She suggested he come over to her apartment for dinner, and Greg quickly accepted.

Greg came into the apartment and at Annie's invitation, walked into her kitchen and opened her refrigerator to get a beer. He gasped in wonder at the dozens of bottles of beer. "You planning on drinking all this by yourself, Annie?"

"Two a night, pal. Two and done. I tried it the other way in college and ruined a few friends' couches before I figured out where my limit was. *Dos para mi, por favor.*"

Greg kept looking at the open refrigerator. "Wait—do I spy some Sam Adams back in there?"

With a fake hurt tone in her voice, Annie answered, "I'm not a chauvinist, Greg. That's a fine American beer. Just like all the other ones in there. What do you want?"

"Dos Equis will be great." Greg paused as she closed the door, after taking out two beers, and then asked, "You're pretty careful with limits and boundaries, aren't you?"

"Yes. Mostly." She handed him his beer.

"What does that mean, mostly?"

"It means mostly, and I decide where my boundaries are." Then Annie heard how over-controlling that sounded, and went on. "With the girls' stuff at work and my sister's stuff back home, I sort of decided I needed to be careful how much I got sucked into all the drama."

"The detached clinician, huh?"

"No! At least I hope not. But I need to make sure I've got something left for myself. That old airline rule: be sure to put on your own oxygen mask first."

She went on. "At first, when Irene went off the rails, I worried that I wasn't doing enough—that none of us were doing enough to rescue her. That there was some therapy or some magic place or some vitamin supplements that would make a difference. But then I finally figured out that all we could do was to make sure Irene knew we were there waiting when she finally decided to turn her life around. And that we couldn't do it for her."

She was quiet for a few moments, and then added, "But I still hate hearing myself say that."

She served dinner, and Greg was suitably impressed with her mother's tamales and corn bread. As they began eating, Annie said, "I need to talk to you about something. Do you remember your lecture on outcomes?" She went on and told him about her "study." Then she said "You see, you inspired me with that lecture."

Greg smiled and said, "There were some repercussions. Raising the issue of cooked outcomes is painful in residential programs. And I was told by my supervisor that Suzanne had called him and suggested that I was asking the wrong questions in the wrong way. She was not happy."

Annie then briefed Greg on her phone calls to former graduates. Greg was amazed. "You called them—how many?

"Thirty who were enrolled here over the past five years. I've only located twenty of them so far."

'Well, Suzanne's right. What you're doing isn't science—but it is sure as hell powerful. Good for you. I can see why Suzanne is shaken up."

Recalling her latest session with Suzanne, Annie suspected that Suzanne was feeling even more pressure than usual in light of the pending acquisition. Annie was certain that the pressure on Suzanne was behind her nervousness about the negative results from Annie's phone calls. She mentioned this, and Greg said, "We've heard those rumors, too, but no one knows when it's going to happen."

Annie said "From what she told me, it's going to happen very soon. They're getting ready to lay off staff in the houses right away."

Greg shook his head. "That sure won't improve any of those outcomes. If you have even fewer staff working with the girls, and if they eliminate your part of the therapy, it cuts the dosage all the more. It's like prescribing antibiotics and then letting the patient take one or two and throw the rest away. Too little dosage to make a difference."

It was a quiet evening, with a lot of talk about work, and a little about each other. It ended with Greg giving Annie a hug and a modest, almost brotherly kiss. Annie could see that Greg was a slow mover, and she decided she would test her own patience. For a while.

25

Lexie

The first snow had fallen back up in the mountains, and Sue announced to all of us in Prospect that we were going to take a snow trip next weekend. A good skiing area was less than two hours drive from The Houses, and most of the girls had been to the snow last winter. I was looking forward to it because I had skied a lot in California.

Saturday morning was clear and sunny, and the trip up to the ski area was full of music and gratitude at skipping the usual Saturday morning deep cleans—if only for a day. The van was big enough to hold all ten girls and two staff members. Kendra and Evelyn had both signed up for the trip—I think they got extra pay or something.

Music that was frowned on in Prospect was allowed in the van, so the girls who had iPod privileges competed for the right to plug in their songs for playing through the van's radio. Somehow, without regular access to radio or MTV, we were able to sing along with nearly every song on anyone's iPod.

I had skied the past winter at June Mountain, where my family usually went, and I thought I was probably in decent enough condition to be able to pick it right up again. Some of the girls had snowboarded before, but only two others had skied with their families as much as I had.

My mom was a serious skier, having grown up in Reno with direct access to the Tahoe ski areas. She had taught me to ski at 4, and as I progressed past her skill level, my uncle and my cousins had spent a lot of time teaching me the finer points of skiing. They were great coaches—two of them were ski instructors at June, and mom always made me take lessons on the first snow trip of the year. My mother told me that the gift of time they'd all given me was one of the nicest gifts anyone had ever given her children.

Justine doesn't ski. She says it's too cold and messes her hair up.

My father is a so-so skier but usually stays back at the house working on files he brings along, or just reading. He once admitted to me that he hates heights.

The van arrived at the resort, we unloaded the snowboards that belonged to The Houses, and four of us went off to rent skis. I was done faster than anyone else and stood with my skis on at the edge of the lift area where I could see the other girls when they came out of the rental shop.

As I watched for them, I looked out at the lift lines, the blue sky, and the sparkling crystals glistening off the snow. It had snowed two days ago, and the sun was shining with a few clouds sliding eastward beyond the top of the mountain.

And all of it gave me a feeling of *I belong here* that I hadn't had for a long time.

Then the rest of them caught up with me. In the midst of snapping on skis and snow boards, I noticed that Monica was having trouble with her skis. I sidestepped over to her and quietly, so no one would hear me, I asked her, "Hey, Monica, can I help you?"

She looked up, embarrassed, and said "Oh yeah, would you? I thought I would try skiing but I have no idea how this stuff works."

So I slipped out of my skis, knelt down and buckled her in. As I stood up, I could tell that she would need help with skiing, not just with the equipment. For a moment I resisted, knowing there would be fast runs I would not get to if I were poking along with Monica. But then I remembered the number of times she had helped me in math class. Monica was the top student in every one of our classes. And I also remembered the great patience of my uncle and my cousins when I was 9 and thought I knew everything about skiing.

Time to pay it back—or something.

"Monica—you have totally lucked out today. Because I am the world's best ski instructor. Follow me, do what I say, and you can't go wrong."

And we had a hell of a good time. I took her over to the bunny slope, which was empty because it was not yet full season. We worked there for an hour or so, until she got her balance. Then we went up the easiest run, and by noon she was riding the ski lift to a medium-green run and having the time of her life.

Monica was at heart a serious nerd, but as I watched her, the quiet, short girl who always knew the answers had morphed into a skier who, like Tom Cruise in *Top Gun*, had a fierce "need for speed."

It felt great. I watched her make a run that would have terrified her two hours before. And then somehow the idea popped into my head that I had never had a black dog day in the mountains, and had never been depressed when I was skiing.

Maybe I should move to the mountains.

Holly and I were taking a break at the lodge. Holly was one of the real skiers, whose family had a condo at Mammoth, so she was very good. She was sort of quiet, and I hadn't gotten to know her very well. In group a few times she talked about her father who had died a few years before Holly began to "fall apart," as she phrased it.

We were sitting at a table on the second level of the ski lodge. At the next table a father was having a late breakfast with his daughter, and he was taking pictures of her as she ate. She was about 7 or 8, and was laughing at her father as he kept moving around the table trying to get a better picture.

And then they were finished eating, and picked up their trays, and paused for a moment to look out at the slopes. They had on matching red jackets and yellow ski caps. The girl stood up on the picnic table seat and held onto her dad's arm tightly as they watched the lines on the ski lifts. They just stood like that for a while, talking softly to each other. The little girl was leaning into her dad, with her head on his shoulder.

And I looked over at Holly, who was able to catch the first tear before it got all the way down her face. But then more came, and she stopped trying to wipe them away. And as I walked around the table and gave her a hug, I suddenly missed my dad. A lot.

After lunch I checked back with Monica, and she urged me to keep going on the faster runs, so I left her with some of the beginner snowboarders and Kendra. I was a little anxious about Kendra being in charge, because her sensitivity to girls with different abilities was almost non-existent. But Monica said she would be fine, and so I raced off to the fastest blue runs and then did a black diamond, as the feeling of control of my skis and my body came back.

As I came down the run, I saw Laurie with a snowboard instructor who was yelling at her "Laurie—you have to know how to stop. You need brakes, too."

And suddenly I heard my mother saying "Honey, when you get into one of your black dog mania phases, you need to have strong brakes so you can stop before you hurt somebody verbally or physically."

Brakes—that's what Laurie needed. I guess that's what I needed, too.

I was getting ready to take a breather and go back and sit on the porch of the lodge for a while. I had come down a blue run and was skiing up to the widened area at the bottom of the hill where everyone had to slow down and approach the lifts. And then off to the side, at the edge of the trail, I saw Monica with Kendra leaning over her waving her arms.

I quickly headed over there and as I skidded to a stop—without taking much care whether or not I sprayed Kendra with snow as I stopped, I heard Monica whimpering "Just go away and leave me alone. Can't you please leave me alone?"

"Get up, you worthless little zero," Kendra said. "I'm not going to leave you here and have the ski patrol pick you up and get us in trouble.

You obviously can't handle skis and you never should have tried this run."

As I heard Kendra and saw how upset Monica was, I was furious. "Back off, Kendra. She's doing fine. She worked hard all morning and she knows what she's doing. Leave her alone."

I guess she was amazed that I would take her on—and for several moments, she just stood there with her mouth open.

Monica said, "It's all right, Lexie. I don't want you to get in any trouble."

Kendra had recovered by then and said, "Great advice, Crockett. You're looking at 10,000 negatives for backtalking me."

I started to answer, but just then I saw three snowboarders headed toward us, and as they got closer, I saw that it was Belinda, Laurie, and Amanda. They skidded up and stopped. Belinda took a look at Monica, still lying on the snow, and said "What's happening?"

Kendra snapped, "Nothing that needs to concern you, Belinda. Now turn that board around and get it down the hill."

Then Belinda gave me a funny look and said, automatically, "McQueen or Brynner?"

I quickly answered," Me McQueen, you Brynner."

It was code. Both our fathers were *Magnificent Seven* freaks, and Kendra had just spoken the key line in the classic hearse scene which the two of us had probably seen twenty times as we were growing up. It had become a kind of secret code between us—both funny and sad. For Belinda, it was one of her last memories before her father died.

Then I stepped into Kendra's space and got so close to her she stumbled backward and almost fell. I said, "Kendra, you're way over the line. Now we're going to let you off if you leave Monica and head out."

"You're going to let me off? The whole bunch of you are going to get—"

But she didn't finish the sentence, because Belinda had stepped out of her snowboard clamps and had stepped up as close as I had just done, and said, "Kendra, we're only going to say this once. You are the one going down this hill—right now. Or you're going to get your 10,000 negatives shoved right up where the sun don't shine."

Kendra was at least six inches shorter than Belinda so by this time she was looking up at her with her head tilted back.

And then I moved my arm quickly, not touching her, but looking like I was going to push her, and yelled, "Go! Now! And leave Monica alone!" And as I did it, the other girls took a step toward Kendra, all at the same time.

She stepped back, glared at the five of us for a moment, and then turned around, heading down the hill. I yelled again, "Stop!" and she did, turning around with a glare on her face. And I said "Remember, Kendra, what happens on the mountain stays on the mountain."

And Belinda added, "Or else."

As we watched Kendra ski down the hill, we just stood there. Then we turned and looked at each other. We were both overjoyed and amazed at the small victory. Monica was still speechless at her rescue as she stood up and put her skis back on. Then she finally said. "Wow. Thanks, guys. That was unbelievable."

I knew it would never have happened back at Prospect. But it had happened here, and we won one. What a great feeling; it wasn't just that Kendra backed off—it was that she was totally wrong, and we were right. And right won—for once.

Two weeks later Kendra resigned to go back to school. We had a great party.

26

Annie

When the van came back to Prospect, Annie was in the staff office finishing up some paperwork that she had left for the weekend when she knew it would be quiet. As the girls unloaded the van and came back into the house, Annie sensed more tension than was usual for such a trip. She noticed that Kendra came into the house from the van, picked up her car keys, and immediately left out the front door without speaking to anyone.

And then as the girls came into the house, she saw that they were giggling, and she heard Belinda say "Turn that rig around and get it down the hill!"

And Annie had no idea what was going on. But she had an idea that Kendra had overplayed her hand.

27

Lexie

I was hanging out after school in the family room with Amanda, when Sue came out of the staff office and said "Amanda, there's a call for you. Take it in the office."

Sue and Amanda went back in the office and closed the door. When they came out five minutes or so later, Amanda looked like she'd seen a ghost. She walked slowly over to the couch and sat down next to me.

"What is it? What happened?" I asked her.

"It's my birth mother. She says she's five minutes away and wants to see me. I have to decide if I want to."

"When's the last time you saw her?"

"Fifteen years ago, I guess, when she left me in the hospital."

Amanda had been adopted, like three of the other girls in our house. She'd mentioned it in group, but she seemed to be one of the people who had gotten past the confusion every adopted kid has about not being wanted and still wondering where her birth parents are. But now she looked really scared.

"What can I say to her, Lexie?"

"Seems like she's the one with things she needs to say. Just tell her the truth." I knew I wasn't much of a counselor, but that was the best I could do. "Do you want to see her?"

"I don't know. I guess so, just to get it over with. She's here, she came all the way from California, so I should see her. My parents have always said it's my decision if I want to get in touch with her—but I never wanted to." She was trying to convince herself, and trying to be a decent kid about it, too. Then she turned to me and said, "Lexie, will you stay with me while I talk to her? I'd feel so much better if someone I trust was with me."

How do you turn down a friend who asks that kind of favor?

"Sure, if you want me to. I'll see her with you."

She hugged me, and we sat waiting for the doorbell to ring.

It was at least half an hour—she may have been five minutes away but she either got lost or had her own fears about the meeting. But then the doorbell rang. Amanda was shaking by then. We got up, with me holding her hand, and we went out to the door with Sue.

Sue opened the door, and right away I could see that this woman was Amanda's birth mother—and that she was a wreck. She had Amanda's round, pretty face, but it hadn't been pretty for a long time.

I know what meth teeth are. I had seen them on the parents of some of my more scumbag friends. This woman had a bad set of them, along with the sunken eyes and bad skin of a serious meth user. Past her in the driveway I could see a Harley, with a fat guy sitting on it in a wife-beater T-shirt under a leather jacket.

She stepped into the house. "Amanda, I'm your mother." And she awkwardly moved to hug her. Amanda gave her one of the arms-only hugs you give a distant aunt, and stepped back.

Sue, PITA as always, said "If you'd like to come in, you can talk with Amanda and her friend in the front room. Amanda has asked that her friend Lexie stay with her. I'm afraid you only have a half hour. It's hard to fit this into the girls' schedule without an appointment."

Amanda's mom, whose name turned out to be Tammy, glared at Sue. "Fifteen years, I come a thousand miles, and I get half an hour?"

Sue stayed in tight-ass mode. "Perhaps next time you can make an appointment and stay longer."

We went into the front room and sat down. Amanda had said nothing, just stared at Tammy.

Tammy looked back at her, and tried to smile. The teeth didn't help. "You're smart, aren't you? And you like to draw. And you dance."

"How did you know that?"

"Because I gave it to you. I may have messed you up, but I did you some good, baby. I really did you some good. People have always told me I was smart, and I never paid enough attention to it. Don't throw that away—use your brains and your eyes to see how to draw things."

She was saying all this in a rushed voice, words just tumbling out of her mouth.

Amanda asked her, with an angry look on her face, "Why are you here? After all these freakin' years, why are you here?"

"I heard from your adoptive parents that you were here, and it made me so mad that they had put you here, I convinced my friend—" she motioned out the window to the biker—"to bring me here. I just . . . I just wanted to see you, and tell you I'm sorry. And I hope maybe I could see you when you get back home to San Diego. I'm living in Oceanside now, in a motel." She paused, realizing she was talking too much. "Could I come and see you when you get home? Rod and Kathleen said I could if it was OK with you. Can I?"

She was like a kid asking permission from her parent to do something. Amanda was quiet, looked at me for a moment, and then said quietly, "Maybe. I need to think about it. I probably get out of here in four or five months. Write me and I'll try to decide."

Tammy was crying now, and said "Thank you. That's all I can ask. I know I messed up my life, and I would have been a bad mother to you. But I'm trying to get better. That's why I came out here. I wanted you to know I'm getting better, and I'd like to see you and be part of your life."

Amanda leaned forward and pointed at her, and said, in words that made me think, again, that she was the parent, "There's no way in hell you are going to see me if you don't get into treatment. You're getting better—great. Get into treatment."

Tammy made a face, but then she nodded. "I will. I've tried it before, but I just couldn't handle it. But I'll try again."

Amanda kept wagging her finger at Tammy. "You've got to do it. It has to come first. I've worked hard here to figure out why I did drugs. And I am not letting anybody—anybody—back into my life who will pull me down again. Understand?"

I was so proud of her. She was drawing the line she needed to draw. She had figured out that she needed to protect herself, not be a nice guy and become Tammy's pal. And it looked to me as if that was exactly what Amanda needed to do—to draw the line and protect herself.

Tammy was nodding in agreement, but with a very worried look on her face. I could tell she was scared, and not at all sure she could do what Amanda was demanding.

When she left, Amanda and I went back into the family room. She looked drained, like she'd just fought ten rounds with a tiger.

"You were great, Mandy. You were so great."

"I don't know. It's going to be hard. Did you hear her about the art and dance and stuff? Can you believe that? She really knows something about me—and I haven't seen her for fifteen years. That totally messed-up looking woman—and she knows all about me." She kept shaking her head, and then asked me, "Can I listen to the night time CD? I need to calm down." She reached over and grabbed my hand. "And Lexie—thanks."

"Sure."

My mother had made me a special CD of some quiet night time music that I used to listen to at home. It had some Jack Johnson, a Charlotte Church CD, some soft guitar music, and some songs by a guy named Harry Nilsson who my parents liked. It was all slow and mellow music, perfect for listening to while falling asleep. The staff let me listen to it if I was on second level and if I kept the CD player turned down very low.

My all-time favorite was a song by Charlotte Church singing about fourteen angels watching over a child as she falls asleep. A few of the girls had gotten to know it, and they asked me to let them make copies of the CD. Amanda loved it, and the first night we listened to it, Amanda said to me sadly "I wish I had fourteen angels watching over me."

And then it turned into a funny thing, as well as a great night-time go-to-sleep tune. Somebody asked me who wrote the fourteen angels song, and I said she didn't remember but thought it was from some opera. I asked my mom on the phone, and when she answered, I thought she was making it up as a joke. Once my mom confirmed it, I couldn't wait to tell the girls.

"Oh, Lexie, you're making that up."

"No, I swear that's the real name."

And so after that, when we were listening to the fourteen angels song, as much as they loved it, sooner or later someone would giggle and softly say "Go, Englebert Humperdinck. Go, you Humper."

28

Annie

Annie had begun working with Lorraine Valdez, a new staff member who was on a graduate internship in Prospect. Lorraine came to the house three days a week, usually after the girls got home from school in mid-afternoon. She stayed until they were in their rooms at night.

Lorraine was finishing her social work degree at the state university, and had a 60-mile round-trip commute from her home to The Houses each day. As Annie interviewed her the first time, Lorraine's eagerness about the work made Annie feel that Lorraine had more potential than any of the other staff. She was tall, just under six feet, and had played basketball at Occidental in Los Angeles where she had graduated two years ago. She had long brown hair like Annie's and a great smile.

Annie had asked her "Why do you want to work here?" Lorraine's answer had been "Because some of these girls aren't going to make it unless they get good help, and I want to become good enough to make a difference to them."

Annie had interviewed dozens of candidates in her five years with the program, and the typical answers were "I like working with teenagers" or "this work will help me get my master's degree." But Lorraine had combined wanting to improve her own skills with hope for the girls' futures in a way Annie had never heard in an interview.

When Annie probed, Lorraine revealed that a cousin she had been close to had recently gone into the state prison system for dealing drugs and attacking her parents. Annie then revealed some of her own family background, and Lorraine relaxed, feeling a bond with Annie. And Annie knew that Lorraine would tune into the girls' wants and needs at a different level than most of the staff could.

So Annie tried to set aside a few minutes each day when her schedule and Lorraine's overlapped to talk with her about the work that day: which girls she had interacted with, how it had gone, how she had handled the points system and how Lorraine read the progress the girls were making.

After a few weeks, Lorraine came into Annie's office and cautiously showed Annie a chart she had made that she carried on her Blackberry. Annie had never seen anything like it; Lorraine had listed each girl, her total points for the past month compared with the points Lorraine had personally given her or taken away, and detailed comments about areas of progress or problems that Lorraine had witnessed. As she reviewed it, Annie saw that Lorraine had developed a tool that enabled her to see how her "grading" of the girls compared with the rest of the staff who were on the same shift. The differences were striking. Lorraine's point awards were consistently higher than the other staff, and her negatives were about half of the rest of them.

After Annie had looked at it, Lorraine explained. "I worry that this shows I'm an easy grader. But, no disrespect or anything, but the other staff seem to mark them down anytime they make the smallest mistake or just forget something. I only take off points if they refuse to do a chore—not if they forget. You know, some of these girls forget a lot. I was thinking maybe that has something to do with their mental ability and damage that may have been done to them. Does that sound right?"

Lorraine had instinctively grasped what some staff of many years could not get—that trauma had cognitive as well as emotional effects on some of the girls. Annie had come to believe that this damage was almost completely ignored by a system that assumed the girls were making rational choices or could be coerced into making rational choices.

Annie nodded and said, "I was watching the staff the other day with the new girl—Sophia? She does something wrong or something they just don't like—5000 points off; she asks why, 2500 more points off for arguing. She uses foul language because they ignore her questions, 5000 more points off. She is escalating every minute, and they have no clue how to cycle her back down, how to disengage or divert her. They just go for the confrontation because that's what a behavioral program does—it punishes questioning as bad behavior. Half the time they can't even tell the difference between a kid grumbling the way all teenagers do when they're asked to do something and when she's losing control and going over the line."

Lorraine said, "I know. I wasn't sure how to handle her when I had to, but I could see what they were doing wasn't working. I read a great book in class last week by a guy from Chicago who works with kids who have been prenatally exposed to drugs. And he said for all the damage done to these kids, sometimes a kid is just a kid."

Then Annie asked Lorraine a question she rarely brought up with the other staff. "What do you think of the behavioral side of our program?"

Lorraine looked at her for a moment and asked her own question. "Is there any other side?"

Annie laughed and said, "I guess that's the point, isn't it? If all we do is behavioral, we sure miss a lot if some of their problems aren't just behavioral." She watched Lorraine to see if she was comfortable talking about the program this way. She went on. "This is just me talking, Lorraine, this is not the program. I spent a lot of time when I first got here trying to figure out just what 'behavioral' means. I heard the other staff saying to parents and to each other 'it's behavioral' when a girl acted out. And I took a long time figuring out what that means. 'It's behavioral' to some of the staff seems to mean that we can fix her if we reward and punish her enough. Like they think somehow she'll just grow new brain wiring every time we give her points or take them away. And then she'll be good for the rest of her life—as long as she hangs around with people who will give her 5000 points when she does the right thing."

She continued, "Or behavioral means the parents messed her up. She's just spoiled and needs so-called boundaries. Or it means she's a high-spirited girl who just needs to be broken and tamed—kind of like one of those horses out there in the field."

Lorraine laughed and said "We were talking about the equine therapy the other day, and Laurie said the funniest thing. She said 'they tell us all the time that the horses can read our emotions. If they're that sensitive, why don't they make them the therapists here and get rid of the staff?'"

Annie laughed and said, "Not a bad question."

Lorraine said, "Something else. I hope this is OK. I mentioned the book I read on prenatal exposure. It really made me think about our girls. So when I was meeting with each of the girls last week, I asked each of them as casually as I could what they knew about their parents' drug use. And Annie, everyone except Laila said that their parents had been pretty heavy drug or alcohol users. Half of them said their parents smoked—way above the national average. And three of them volunteered without my asking that they were pretty sure their mothers had used while they were pregnant. They all had health education in school; they all heard that drugs and alcohol during pregnancy are bad. So most of them went home and asked their moms—except those that already knew and didn't have to ask."

Annie smiled and said, "Great research, Lorraine. What do you make of it?"

Lorraine said, "I'm not sure. But it says to me that the behavioral stuff has a long way to go before it can make a real impact on a brain where the control functions are weak—where the brakes are shot and the accelerator sometimes gets stuck." She laughed. "Call it the Toyota syndrome. But the idea that taking points away can consistently heal a damaged brain is a far stretch, it seems to me."

"Me too," said Annie.

But Lorraine pressed on. "So what do we do if we think it shouldn't be just a behavioral program? What's the alternative?"

Annie reached over and patted her on the knee. "Lorraine, you're asking questions that staff who've been doing this for twenty years never ask. I'm glad you're asking these questions. I wish I had better answers. But for now, I know this much: It is partly how we treat these girls that are here going through what we label 'treatment.' And if we treat them as if they're little robots who we can train to do the right thing with points and punishments, we'll never get through to most of them, and nothing we do will last when they get back home. My friend Greg from headquarters talks about 'dosage" as a big deal—like taking a few antibiotic pills and throwing the bottle away. It just won't work. I'm worried about our dosage—but I'm also worried that it isn't even the right medicine.

"There's a lot of new research now on adult brain plasticity—which is a fancy way to say even adults can keep growing new brain cells and circuits. Thank God, huh? And some people go from that research to saying that adolescents can grow new wiring that helps them control their impulses. And the behavioral people jump on all that and go right away to incentives and sanctions, or points and levels. But what if a girl can't keep the fear of sanctions in the front of her brain, while the certainty of a thrill from drugs or sex or whatever is working on the rest of her brain? Then what?

"Our job is to push these girls, and then pick them up. Force them to think about their futures, not just getting out of here, but where they go next and what they need to do to get there. And at the same time, making sure that they also spend some time thinking about how they got here and how they can stay out of places like this from here on.

"We're always looking for the balance—pushing them and lifting them up after so many people have held them down. It is exhausting, and it is exhilarating. Some days I hate it, and then one little spark will land and I will see a girl starting to get it, see it dawn in her eyes that she finally knows who she could be. It lifts me up for days."

Annie went on, pleased that Lorraine had asked her what she really thought. She knew it was risky to talk to her this way, in case Lorraine repeated to senior staff what she was saying, but she didn't care. "There are girls here who get it the first day they arrive. They want to go home, they'll do whatever it takes to get home, they work the program as hard as they can—and they go home. There are others who want to go home but just can't control themselves or focus well enough to do the work consistently. They get it going, they get to second level, and then they blow up, or they forget the rules, or they just get too tired with all the meds and they refuse to go to class or do the housework. And so they get negatives all the time.

"And then there are the girls who are too frightened to go home. We have to remember that some of these girls are throw-away kids. Their parents never wanted them, never paid any attention to them. And when they started getting in trouble, the parents blamed the girls and just kicked them out. These girls don't want to be here—but some of them have absolutely no other safe place to live.

"I remember there was a girl in one of the houses who had been here for almost two years, and everyone on staff agreed she should go home, that we couldn't do anything more for her. But she was terrified that she would be sent back home. She begged us to let her stay here, she said she couldn't go back with her mother who was on the streets by then. And she didn't know where her father was.

"And so after a lot of back and forth, they set up the new transition program and converted one of the little staff houses into apartments for three girls who needed a place to live and couldn't return home. They got jobs here and stayed here for a year or so and then all three of them moved together into the Phoenix area, I think. We did a good job with those girls—I was proud of our program for adding that piece.

"But for some girls, the calendar screws them. When you hit 18—in most of the states where these girls are from—you're out of school and the funding starts to cut off. And then they have to leave, unless we can get them into the transition program."

She stopped and looked out the window of Prospect to the high desert stretching off to the horizon. "All that land out there. I sometimes wish we could just build a safe place out there for every one of these girls, and let them live there, and run their own little town of girls who got better." She smiled. "We'd need a name for the town. There's a Spanish word but I can't think of it, means 'got better?'"

Lorraine quickly said "*Mejorado?*"

Annie clapped her hands, and said "Perfect. *Mejorado* it is!"

29

Lexie

I walked in the house with four other girls after classes and right away heard somebody screaming. Sue met us at the door and quickly herded us into the kitchen. The screaming was coming from the downstairs front bedroom, and I knew it was Sophia.

"Give me back my fucking meds! You people are trying to kill me! Give me my meds!" And she kept screaming that one phrase over and over, until I heard thumping and a door slam. They had taken her into the back room—the isolation room. I could still hear muffled screams, but the room was sound-insulated, and the screams were very faint.

"What's going on?" Laurie whispered to me.

"I heard Sophia talking to Sue about it last weekend. Those assholes Gustafson and Jolson decided to zero out her meds. They decided that what she was taking wasn't working, so they took her off everything at once to start over with a new combination."

I had heard of the shrinks doing this before. Every psychiatrist has his or her own recipe for fixing our brains, and so sometimes they want to start over with whatever they think will work better. They told one girl in another house that they were going to change her meds because she's too hyper. But all they really did was try to knock her out so she wouldn't be any trouble. For weeks, she walked around like a zombie, falling asleep in every class. Finally they sent her to the psych hospital to try to get the meds straightened out because she had gotten so messed up.

A friend of mine from school whose father was a researcher at UC Irvine said sometimes shrinks do this because they have been paid by the drug manufacturers to test some new drug. So they test it on kids who have been locked up. Like we were some kind of lab animals and they could just switch us from one batch of drugs to another, and then put us back in our cages to see what happens.

Only for Sophia, the cage was isolation.

30

Annie

Annie drove over to Desert City to attend another staff training session. The lecturer was a therapist who had worked at four different centers over forty years. When Greg introduced her, he said that she had gotten nearly every award that the RTC field could give. She was short, looked to be in her late sixties, and had close-cropped grey hair. Her smile was quite remarkable; it lit up her whole face and came with an involuntary nodding that made her seem like a happy version of a bobble-headed handout at a baseball game. Her name was Marianne Linsky.

She arranged some files on the lectern, and lowered her head for a moment. Then she lifted it, and began by talking about therapy and the different fads in therapy she had seen in her decades of work in the field. She had a faintly Germanic accent, with a formal way of speaking and then pausing for the points to sink in.

She began by saying that she had little patience for the theorists of residential treatment. She said that "listening to these kids and finding something to like about them" was the key to good therapy, not sticking to a theoretical construct. Then she talked about what she called "the myth of therapeutic breakthroughs." Annie listened, fascinated.

"When these kids make progress, it's usually not some big breakthrough in therapy that brings it on. They get better, when they do, in small pieces. They get interested in something besides themselves, they realize they're good at something, they meet the right kid, or they see the wrong kid getting in serious trouble. Sometimes they just get a hell of a good scare—they see how someone who makes bad choices really has to live, on the streets, dirty and broke—and they realize that they don't want to live that way. They walk away from a car wreck, or they wake up in a hospital from an overdose. Or they lose a friend who didn't wake up. The adopted ones see how far down their birth parents have fallen, and they wake up to the fact that they don't have to go down there. They begin to believe that the circle can be broken with them.

"And sometimes—just sometimes—a place like ours makes a difference. A good therapist works an inch at a time, and maybe she gets to a point where the kid sees something or hears something, And then, blessedly, you know you've gotten through. But it doesn't come by magic, it comes by putting your butt in that chair and listening.

"It's hard to admit, when you see all the paper on our walls, all those diplomas and certificates of this and that, but sometimes the best therapists in places like RTCs are the kids themselves. I've seen girls suddenly straighten up in group therapy and stare at another girl after she says something ordinary. That girl just heard something for the first time—something I may have said a dozen times and never gotten through. They listen to each other on a different frequency than they listen to us, and more gets through when they really tune in to each other than when we are droning on at them.

"We need to listen, and we need to learn to watch them, to watch their faces. We need to watch the faces of these girls, see them when they sit at the big table for dinner, see them studying in the library between classes, see them out on the soccer fields and riding horses. They're confused, some of them, angry—most of them. They watch you to see if you are going to bring them more grief or some comfort. They've learned to read us very carefully. Some of them look younger than they are, seeming twelve or thirteen, and others are already hard-faced, worn down by what they've been through."

She looked down at the files, pushed them a few inches away from her. "And every one of them, no matter what they did to get sent here, deserves our best. We don't always give it to them, either. We get impatient, they irritate us, we stop looking for what they're good at, and we give up on them. And they know it, because someone else has already given up on most of them. They know what that looks like, and what it feels like. And with a little bit of carelessness or irritation, we can bring that rotten memory surging back up to the surface of that girl's emotions. And every time that happens to one of them, a little bit of what that girl could be just dies. We're supposed to be giving them a better life, and sometimes all we do is kill them a little bit.

"How can we send one of these girls to a locked-down program that will throw her into isolation and leave her there for days? You take a girl with mental illness who trusts no one and you toss her in isolation—in a cell, basically—when she acts out. And most of them will get worse, sicker and sicker. And so angry at us and herself that she finally snaps. And tries to kill herself or hurt someone else so badly she'll finally get kicked out.

"And we call that therapy? We call that treatment? How dare we?"

She was looking at them with a frown, and Annie could hear how deeply critical she was of how some therapists and staff operated. Annie had never heard anybody ever talk about the work that way.

"And we need to remember all that has happened to these girls and how much some of them have been marked by what happened to them before they were born. Prenatal drugs, alcohol, and tobacco brought us many of these girls. We've all learned through the brain science of the last decade how to talk about executive functioning and the prefrontal cortex. But what that means in our programs is that we sometimes use so-called behavioral approaches as if giving points or taking them away could magically create new synapses in brains that have very few brakes."

By now Annie was replaying her conversation with Lorraine of a few days earlier.

Marianne looked out at the audience and smiled her great smile again, though this time it was to soften what was coming. "And we also

133

need to know how to deal with the science of it all. I mean no disrespect to researchers and the biochemical pharmo folks—" she paused for the laughter to die down, "but we need to know what they do and don't know. For all that we know now about brain science and CAT Scans and PET scans and all that—and all that the pharmo people know about new meds—we're still just beginning to move out of witchcraft. In my experience, most of the time the shrinks are just guessing with meds. And the best of them admit it—the rest just fake knowing. The side effects are terrible with some of these concoctions, and yet we put four or five of them together in a cup and give them to these kids twice a day. And we have no idea what the combinations of all these meds do—no idea at all about how they interact. The good news is that the science is moving in the right direction, but the bad news is that it is still moving too slow to make a difference for a lot of these girls.

"The meds matter—I'm not saying they don't matter. But it is the whole program that makes a difference if it's any good, and the parents, and what the girl herself can bring to the job. The program, the parents, and the girls. And the meds are supposed to help the girls bring their best selves to the work, and give them time to build on their best instincts and slow down their worst impulses.

"And I cannot let the opportunity go by to mention medication abuse—drug abuse, if you will. What I mean is drug abuse by the professionals prescribing drugs to these girls."

The audience had visibly frozen, as she had expected. Annie suspected many of them were shocked that she was venturing into such a controversial area. She saw Dr. Gustafson and Dr. Jolson sitting with their colleagues from the university, who all had well-paid, part-time psychiatric staff positions with The Houses, and noticed Jolson looking around at his seatmates, shaking his head and frowning.

Marianne continued. "Now, I am not some holistic, herbalist nut case. I believe medications can help these girls, and I have seen some lives saved by good medications management. But there isn't a single person in this room who would not admit—if you were being totally honest—that you don't know of lots of cases in which the purpose of medications was not stronger impulse control, but in fact stronger sedation. A sleepy girl is a docile girl, and makes less trouble. That saves money.

"We have a raft of studies coming from the long-term care industry that lay out how often we sedate the elderly to keep them less troublesome in nursing homes. It's cheaper by far to overdose them than if they were all flipping out all the time with the confusion of dementia. There are court cases pending in this country right now about nursing homes that have over-sedated their residents, and there will be more as boomers retire and some start wondering what is happening to their parents—and to some of their spouses and friends. There are also cases in which prisons, especially the private ones, use psychotropic drugs widely to calm inmates, and the Supreme Court has expanded prisons' legal rights to force inmates to take them.

"So that brings us back to these girls. I'm not going to ask for a show of hands as to how many of you have resisted prescribing meds for girls that were intended to tranquilize them instead of helping them get control of their lives." She smiled. "But I could. And I'm not going to ask how many of the distinguished psychological and psychiatric practitioners here have refused reimbursement from pharmaceutical firms who offered funding if you would track use of their products on these girls." This time she didn't smile. "But I could."

"I have no problem using medications to calm a girl down who is agitated and potentially dangerous. But you and I know that in some facilities these drugs are over-used, used as punishment, and used to make things easier for the staff. And that's wrong."

At this point, Gustafson, Jolson, and Co. were working hard to seem totally disinterested in what Marianne was saying, looking at their watches, leafing through their briefcases, or playing with their Blackberries.

Marianne paused long enough to make clear that she was moving on to another topic.

"And then, out beyond the science and the meds and the therapy, is grace. Now I'm not here to give a sermon, but the scientists have learned a lot in the last few decades about the spiritual side of mental illness, and I encourage you to read that literature if you want to know more about it."

She was quiet, closed her eyes for a second, then said "Here is what I believe, for what it is worth. Every one of these girls needs to be prayed for. And there are a dozen different ways to pray for them. For some of you, the best way to pray will simply be being good to them, to be better to them than they seem to deserve when they are cursing you or ignoring you. To forgive them when they curse you, to know what they have been through, and to know that all of them are still God's children while they are here in our care and when we try to prepare them to go back home—when they have a home to go to . . ."

"And another thing we sometimes forget. Do not feel too sorry for these girls." She paused and let the statement sink in, watching her audience as carefully as they were watching her. Then she continued, leaning forward, her slight body framed by her rapidly gesturing hands.

"As hard as they have it, they have already come through a lot, most of them. And we deny how strong they are if we make them think of themselves as victims. And we also may undercut them as they do the work of reshaping their own lives, in the face of the disorders or the parental damage they have lived through.

"So don't feel too sorry for them. Watch for their victories, and stay away from too many stories of victims. We need these girls to be winners—not whiners."

Annie didn't care much for the slogans, but she thought there was a lot of truth in the warning about undercutting the girls by framing their lives as victims. The message, Anne knew, wasn't the same thing as the mindless slogan of "tough love." Annie had once heard a psychologist in a state hospital tell adoptive parents that when their adoptive daughter acted up and got thrown in jail just before they were going on a long-postponed vacation, they should have resorted to tough love and gone on the vacation. "And just left her in jail?! Thank God you don't have to raise one of these kids!" the incredulous mother had screamed at the psychologist before storming out of her office.

Marianne shook her head and got a serious look on her face. "And we also need to remember that the girls and boys in most of our centers aren't the saddest kids. As much trouble as these kids have seen and lived through, the saddest places are the next circles of hell down. The fire setters, the sexual predators, the abusers who've been terribly traumatized and are passing the disease on to weaker kids—those are the saddest and the scariest kids. I could never work with kids like that, and the patience of people who do is unbelievable. If we make progress by inches—they make it by millimeters. Tiny, tiny gains. Taking fire setters to burn clinics and trying to get them to connect matches with all that scar tissue—" she shuddered, "now that's heavy lifting. The people who do that work are the real heavyweights in our field."

Then she opened the floor to questions.

A counselor from one of the other Houses asked, "What about meditation? I've read that some programs are using what they call 'mindfulness' techniques. Are they any good?"

"Thanks for the question. I've spent some time looking at those approaches, and if the staff using them are properly trained, they can make a real difference. It essentially combines meditation with cognitive therapy, and for girls with depression symptoms, it can help a lot. You can get workshops on the mindfulness approach through your national organization or through several companies that offer training.

"We are so deeply based in Western traditions of medical practice that we haven't done enough to understand how much wisdom Eastern ideas offer about mind-body connections. What I find remarkable is how much the science behind these approaches is approaching what neuroscience is beginning to finally tell us about the brain. Our girls all need greater mindfulness, because their brains have been traumatized and they have shut down so much. Waking up their brains with meditation could be a very important change in our therapies—and it will demand that all of us make some big changes ourselves."

The Gustafson/Jolson section members were now blatantly BlackBerrying their disdain. And finally Marianne decided to take notice of their rudeness. She gently said "After all, not all the world's wisdom can be contained in a Blackberry—even with extra memory chips."

Afterwards, processing it with Greg, Annie couldn't stop talking about what Marianne had said. "She just cut through all the BS, all of it. She made more sense than any teacher I ever had. She ought to just get in an RV and get a driver and go from program to program, giving that lecture over and over."

Greg laughed, and said "So I picked a good one?"

"You picked her? I thought Administration chose these people who come in and do these lectures."

"No, I chose her. And I got hassled a bit for doing it. What she says about drugs isn't exactly popular among the drug companies—who are big contributors, in case you haven't read the plaques out in the lobby. And psychiatrists aren't all that enthused about her talking about shrinks, either."

"You did good. You need a reward. Ice cream, on me?"

"That's a start."

31

Lexie

Our English teacher was a kind of mousy little woman who was about 40 and who didn't open up very much to us. She was OK, but she sometimes had a hard time keeping the class interesting.

This week she had assigned us to read sections from longer books by this Russian writer, Solzhenitsyn. We had to read part of a book about a prisoner named Ivan Denisovich and some chapters from his longer book *The Gulag Archipelago*. It was hard going, but I thought the way he described life in prison was amazing. You could almost feel what it was like to be in that awful place.

The teacher, Dr. Kelos, was from Hungary or somewhere in Europe, and she had a little bit of an accent. After we all came in and sat down, she said, "We're going to talk today about Alexander Solzhenitsyn who wrote the selections from Ivan Denisovitch and *The Gulag Archipelago* that you read this week. A famous American diplomat, George Kennan, said that the Gulag book was 'the most powerful single indictment of a political regime ever to be levied in modern times.' It showed how prisons were used to control dissent in the Soviet Union and what prisons can do to people." She paused and looked at the class. "What did you think of the book?"

I was pretty sure that Dr. Kelos knew that of the twelve girls in the classroom only four or five of us had actually read the selections from the book. But she seemed determined to see what we had gotten out of it. We were all quiet for a few moments, and then Monica spoke up.

"I was sorry for the prisoners, but what really got me was the guards."

"Why?"

"Some of the guards were sadistic, and some were decent. You did not have to be brutal as a guard, but some of them liked having the power and used all of their authority to beat down the prisoners. And others tried to make life in the camps a tiny bit better with extra food or lighter punishments or breaks from the hard labor."

Monica was into it. She nearly always did the reading and had a lot to say. She went on. "But the guards had almost total control. They could punish you for the slightest infraction of the rules—or for what they accused you of, whether you really did it or not. They created a world in which they could say a prisoner did something and it became real—just because they said it. They could double the prisoners' sentences, get them sent to isolation, or get them beaten, just because they said it happened. They created reality, and the prisoners—the zeks—lost any hold on their own lives because their words had lost all power to say what we—I mean what they really did."

Everyone heard the slip, and everyone waited to see what Kelos would do.

"But why did the guards interest you so much?"

Very slowly, nervously, Monica said "It kind of reminded me of the staff here. Some are like that."

Kelos gently challenged her. "Are you saying they're like prison guards? Are you saying this is a prison?"

"No. But I'm saying," she paused, and I could tell she was trying to choose her words more carefully than we usually did in class, "I'm saying they have that kind of power—if they say something happened, it happened, whether it's real or not. They have the power to make it real or to say it never happened. If they say I was defiant and refused to accept discipline, then they can take the points away from me, whatever I say, whatever really happened. They can create reality, like the books said the prison guards could."

"That's right," Kelos said. "Now let me be clear. I'm going to talk about the book, not what happens here. Monica, you're right. What Solzhenitsyn was trying to show, I think, was a total loss of freedom. The guards had total power, and for someone to have that kind of control over you is a total loss of freedom. Your words and actions are no longer your reality, because someone else defines you and punishes you based on their power to say what you did, not based on your own actions.

"And after a while, if you are not very sure of yourself to start with, you begin to believe that you really don't deserve the power to run your own life. It chips away at your sense of confidence. The guards' behavior undermines your belief in yourself."

Laurie jumped in, angry, talking faster and faster. "And they pick favorites. And then they drop them and get new ones when someone else comes. They have the power to pick their favorite girl and they make that girl's jobs easier or they change the rotation so they get a day off. And they go into their rooms at night and talk to them." She was near crying now, as the others held their breath and looked anywhere but at Laurie. "There used to be a staff person here—she's gone now—and she would go into another girl's room, and brush her hair for a long time. You could hear them talking softly, and laughing together." She paused, and then blurted out, "And it made the rest of us feel like shit!"

Dr. Kelos knew that Laurie was not talking about the book any more. And then I knew that she also expected that we would see the connection when she assigned these books.

Kelos said, "Look, I'm not going to pass judgment in any way on how the staff here treats you. I'm not in your houses, I don't know most of the staff, and it's not my area. But what I do want to respect is your feelings as you think about what happens to you in a treatment facility. It's not a prison, but it has rules and consequences for breaking those rules. And the staff gets to interpret those rules."

I spoke up, thinking about the debate class. "Like a judge and jury."

"Yes, they sometimes interpret the rules the way a judge does."

Laurie said "For eight dollars an hour, they get to be our judges. How is that fair?"

Kelos answered, "Perhaps that could be something to discuss in one of your group sessions." She paused, letting that idea sink in. Then she asked another question.

"One last point: Anybody have any idea how many Americans are in prisons right now?"

No answer.

"Almost 2½ million people—more in number and percentage than any other nation on earth. Almost one percent of the population. One study in California said that two-thirds of the ones we release end up back in prison within three years. So prisons don't seem to work too well. China is a totalitarian country, in many ways, but it locks up its citizens at only one-fifth the rate we do. The Soviet gulags, in a smaller country, locked up nearly four million people over a period of decades. In a much bigger country, we lock up 2½ million right now." She looked at us, saw that the same four or five of us were still tuned in, and wrapped up: "Something to think about."

32

Annie

Annie was working in the office on a staffing chart when Sue stuck her head in and said "There's a call for you on our phone. I don't know why they didn't use the main number. Take it in here," and she handed me her cellphone.

Annie picked it up, said hello, and listened. She could hear a faint breathing sound and was about to hang up when a very ragged voice said "Annie? That you, baby girl?"

It was Irene. Every time she did this, over the five years since Annie had seen her last, it felt like a punch in the stomach. She gasped and said "Irene, oh, I am so glad you called. How are you doing, big sister?"

"A little better. I have a part-time job now, and I'm out of the shelter and have my own place with some other girls I met in rehab. I made it through two months this time, Annie."

"Good for you." Annie knew better than to ask her what kind of treatment for which kind of drug. That she had hung in for two months was a miracle by itself.

"When are you coming home, Annie?"

"I can come any time. It's a little crazy here now, and I'd love to get away and come see you."

"Well, I don't want to be any trouble."

"Get serious. You're only trouble when you stay away, Irene."

She was quiet, and then Annie heard her say, "You know, Annie, I did a lot of thinking in rehab this time. I thought about what you've always said to me. I need the help. I can't do it alone. I really get it now—you're working with those girls because you know you can help them, some of them anyway."

Annie wiped away a tear, trying to keep her sorrow out of her voice. "That's right, Reny, they need help. It's all right to ask for help."

Irene laughed softly. "Reny. No one has called me Reny for a long time. I miss you, Annie."

"I miss you too," making an instant plan, Annie said, "and I'll be home next week—you keep going a day at a time and I'll see you next week."

33

Lexie

I had been in the bathroom and when I came out everyone had already left for class. I headed downstairs, but then I heard yelling down the hall and could tell that Sophia was still in her room and someone was in there with her. I walked down the hall and looked in. A staff member I didn't recognize at first was standing over Sophia's bed shouting at her "Get up and get your ass to class right now, Sophia. Now!"

It was Tricia somebody from one of the other houses, who had been filling in for Sue while she and Sam were on leave.

Sophia was still in bed, and said "I told you I don't feel good and I'm not going to class. Now get the hell out of here and leave me alone."

Tricia leaned over the bed and started to pull Sophia's arm. Sophia began screaming louder, "Leave me alone."

I yelled at Tricia, "Let her stay there, you're just making it worse, she's going to blow up!"

Tricia ignored me and then pressed a button on her cell phone which I had seen them use before as a panic alert. Within fifteen seconds I heard the front door bang open and Roger Lockyer, one of the security guys, came running up the stairs. He burst into the room, and Tricia said "Get her up, she's going to isolation."

Roger reached down and jerked Sophia up out of bed in her pajamas, and slung her up against the door. "Let's go, kid, downstairs to isolation."

Tricia pointed at me. "Get her too, she was with her." I tried to explain, but Roger had not seen any of it happen, and he just assumed from what Tricia said that I was part of the confrontation with Sophia. So he grabbed me too.

They took us into the back room in the house. It had one small window with bars, a ratty looking old couch, and a mattress on the floor with an old blanket thrown on it. There was a bathroom off to the side that was locked. This was the room no one ever went into because they called it "the secure room" where they took girls when they flipped out

And that is exactly what happened once Sophia got in there. She started kicking the wall, and when Tricia tried to stop her, Sophia swung at her and then spat at her. "Get away from me, you fat bitch!"

I sat down on the floor in the far corner of the room, trying to stay out of range. By this time Evelyn was in the room, and she was sitting on Sophia, who was on the floor, struggling against the three of them, cursing them and spitting whenever they took their hands off her mouth. She had tried to bite Roger, so he was using a towel on her mouth.

I screamed "You're going to choke her!" and Tricia turned and hissed at me, "Shut up unless you want what she's getting."

And then Annie came in the room and it was like some kind of invisible sedative had been sprayed in the air. Sophia had been tensed, getting ready to swing at the staff again. She saw Annie, and she let her arms drop to the mattress. And Annie smiled at her, kind of sad, and said "Rough day, huh, Sophia?"

The rest of the staff had rolled off Sophia when they saw her start to calm, but were still bunched up by the door, and Tricia kept mumbling we should just have her arrested, get her the hell out of here. But Annie ignored them and said "It's OK, Sophia, do you want to calm down and talk about it?"

"I don't want to talk about nothing with these bitches. I want out of here. Now. Right now!"

Annie kept talking with her in that soft voice, but with a tone that said she was still the boss. "We all want out of here, Sophia, this is a crummy room. Let's calm down and see what we can do to get you out of here."

"I want out of here now—I want to leave this shithole now. Make them let me go."

Annie turned and said "Could all the staff wait outside while I talk with Sophia?" She looked at Sophia and said "Do you want Lexie to go or stay?"

She glared at me and then seemed to see who I was. "She can stay."

Roger had left, and so had Evelyn. But Tricia was furious at Annie, and said "She should be arrested, Annie, she assaulted us, and we should call the sheriff and get her out of here right now."

Annie snapped at her, "We're not going to call the sheriff, Tricia. Go read the procedures you were given when you were hired—that's not what we do here. Now please leave before I have to report you."

Tricia moved to the door, saying "I'm going to call Suzanne."

"Please do. And when you do, be sure to tell her that you wanted to violate procedures and let the sheriff take over what we're being paid to do here as professionals. And remind her that I argued against zeroing out Sophia's meds last week in treatment team."

After Tricia shut the door, hard, Annie went over to Sophia, who had crawled over to the mattress that was on the floor. Sophia was quietly sobbing, and saying, almost to herself, "I just want to get out of here. I just want to go home."

Gently, Annie knelt down next to the mattress, reached over, and began rubbing Sophia's head. "It'll be OK, we can work it out. Just relax now, they're gone, you can relax." Annie kept rubbing her head, and I could see Sophia unclenching her fists and sliding her legs down into the blanket covering the mattress.

We stayed like that for five or ten minutes, and finally Sophia went to sleep. Annie motioned to me and we quietly went over and sat on the couch.

Annie said to me, "Thanks for staying. I know you've tried to help her, she's told me, and I think it was good that you could be here and keep it from being just a staff-girl thing." She went on, talking to me but looking out the window where it had started to rain.

"Sometimes staff sets these girls off without needing to. God knows they get set off by the smallest things anyway, but we shouldn't make it worse by provoking them until they blow up and then not knowing how to calm them down. I've seen it happen way too many times." And then she seemed to realize she was talking to me like I was staff and not one of the girls. "Sorry, I didn't mean to air our laundry. Forget I said that."

"Sure, Annie."

But it wasn't over. Tricia had reported me as an "SV"—serious violation. That meant that I lost all privileges for at least three days, with a staff review then deciding how much longer the penalty would continue. Tricia had lost out in her confrontation with Annie, and so I guess she had turned her anger on me. It was just like what the girls had been talking about in class about the Russian camps. The staff said something happened, one of us said it didn't, and it was almost always their word over ours.

I went to Annie, but she said there was nothing she could do about it because she hadn't been there when the whole thing started. Of course Roger backed Tricia. So I was screwed.

34

Annie

Annie hated staff meetings. Few things depressed her more than arguing for hours about brands of cereal and security alarms and phone call timers and all the other petty crap that goes into running a secure program. She knew that somebody needed to worry about tight controls on the girls, most of whom were highly inventive "customers" who loved to challenge authority and bend the rules whenever they could. She just didn't want to be the one who had to worry about those controls.

And Annie almost always walked out of those meetings feeling that some of the staff needed as much counseling as the girls. After the blowup with Sophia, she felt that more than ever.

Deborah Wong ran the meetings as the on-site supervisor. For a while, the educational staff had attended house staff meetings, but it hadn't worked out schedule-wise, and they stopped coming.

There was a sign up in the classroom in Prospect that said "An integrated program for an integrated girl: home, classroom, therapy." But the three pieces of the program at Prospect rarely came together, in Annie's experience. As a result, each girl was fragmented into separate slices, and most of the time, each staff unit worked on their slice separately. In five years of Annie's time at Prospect, there had never been a meeting when the ten girls were discussed by the house staff, the teachers, and the therapists all meeting in one room. Never.

Annie knew this meeting would be much more heated than usual because the coming staff changes were on the agenda. Deborah began the meeting with a little speech she had obviously rehearsed—or been ordered to give.

"As some of you have already heard, the new owners of The Houses will be making some changes. We're going to talk about some of those today." She went on to explain that one staff person would be laid off, Annie's therapy duties would be reduced so she could spend more time in a supervisory role, and other changes would be announced in a few weeks.

The staff were quiet, mostly shocked, it seemed to Annie. Then Sue spoke up and asked "Well, who is it going to be? Who's getting laid off?"

Deborah said "That hasn't been decided yet. But seniority," she avoided looking at Evelyn, the last staff member hired, "and educational plans will factor into the decision.

"What do you mean, educational plans?" Evelyn asked.

"Some of you have talked about going back and getting your master's degrees. If you choose to do that, there is some discussion of the agency giving you some kind of partial scholarship."

Evelyn shot back, "How partial—500 bucks?" She was furious and scared.

"That hasn't been decided yet."

The discussion went on for another half hour, inconclusively, and then the staff left, whispering angrily to each other. Annie thought that at least some of the staff were probably feeling as powerless as the girls sometimes felt. And she wondered if that was entirely a bad thing.

After the meeting, Annie drove into Desert City and caught a flight to Orange County. She wasn't sure she could connect with Irene, but she owed her a try, and she could catch up with her sisters and her parents whether she saw Irene or not. The strain of the changes with the new owners was starting to get to her, and she knew she needed a break.

She usually stayed with Beatrice, who had a larger apartment and was involved with a co-worker whom she often stayed with overnight.

When Bea picked her up, Annie got in the car and said "What's up, sis?"

Bea gave her a strange look and said, "You won't believe it, Annie. Guess who's waiting to have dinner with us at Mom and Dad's?"

Annie put her hands to her face and started crying. "Irene? Oh my God, Irene came home for dinner? Oh, how great—hurry, hurry, get home!"

And Bea, driving fast but carefully, got her home for one of the best meals Annie could remember. Irene was quiet, but mostly smiling. And the rest of the family was overjoyed, trying not to make too much of it, but at the same time hoping that it was the first of more meals with the whole family together—for the first time in ten years.

35

Lexie

Horses weren't a very big deal in my life, until I got to Prospect. But horses are a big deal at The Houses. They have this fancy name, equine therapy, which I guess means you learn to work with a horse and you learn something about yourself.

Great theory. Except the idea was that this half-ton of animal was somehow going to do what a little 110-pound girl wanted it to—instead of what the horse wanted to do.

Right. Same old story—we're "in control"—except when we're not.

The first time I went out to the corral, a week after I got to Prospect, I was terrified. I had seen the other girls out riding in the corral, and some of them made it look fairly easy. But the last time I had been on a horse, it was a little pony at the county fair, I was five, and my dad held my hand during the entire ride, walking around and around in a circle no more than thirty feet across.

The corral was about 150 feet long, and it had barrels in the middle of it. As I watched the other girls riding, I saw that the object was to make the horse go around and through those barrels without hitting any of them—and without going too slow. I had no idea how I was going to do it.

But then it turned out that you don't get to ride the horse until you know more about the horse. So you have to comb its hair, and feed it, and muck out its stall—which is a fancy way of saying you get to shovel a lot of horse shit.

And this is helping me how?

But I did it. I didn't love it, but I did it. Finally comes the day when you get up on the horse, and the horse walks around with you a little bit, and you're riding (or at least walking).

I tried not to let myself get carried away, but it really was pretty awesome. You're up there, about five feet higher than you're used to being, and this very large animal is going where you want it to.

Sometimes. But sometimes he still goes where he wants to, even when you're pulling like crazy on the reins to try to change his mind.

The horse handler, Ford Burnside, was probably the best single person I met while I was at The Houses. He really knew the horses, and he was so patient with the girls. Some of them were much bigger klutzes than I was, and a few were frightened to death of the horses. He said over and over "you have to show the horse that you are in charge," and if you paid attention to him, he also showed you how to do it.

During the last time my parents visited me, I had gotten pretty good at riding, and I took them both down to the corral to show them. Ford put me up on one of the easy horses, Tinker, and I trotted around, at one point going so fast I even scared myself.

My mother wants nothing to do with horses, and my dad had been around horses on pack trips in the Sierra, but never for very long. They were both amazed at what I could do. That day they took some of my favorite photos from Prospect: me riding Tinker, the hills in the background, going around and between the barrels. I looked like I was in charge. It was a good feeling.

Then a few weeks later, I was up on one of the horses and I began to feel my old itch to run—the impulse to take off that had gotten me into so much trouble. I leaned over to Laurie, who was next to me and was one of the best riders.

"Laurie, what's to stop us from riding one of these horses out of the corral and down the road? We wouldn't have to sneak away from here in the night—we could just ride a horse away!"

She shook her head and pointed at the horse's head. "Look at his right ear."

I looked down and there was a little bump on the edge of the horse's ear. I leaned over and felt it. There was a hard knot just under the skin. I looked over and saw that Laurie's horse had the same bump. "What is that?"

"They chip 'em."

"Huh?"

"It's a microchip, like they use for dogs so you can find them if they stray away from home. They started doing it to prevent rustling and now they do it to prevent us from riding away."

"Oh." I shrugged. "There goes my dream of being a cowboy."

36

Annie

Each year an inspector comes out from the state agency that regulates The Houses to make sure the program is in compliance with all the state and federal regulations required when programs get federal funding. The state inspector had overseen The Houses for several years, and Deborah Wong had assigned Annie to handle the visit because she had gotten to know the inspector, Phyllis Norcross.

Phyllis had been to the central office in Desert City and had met with the staff in two of the other houses. Today was her last day of the visit. Annie met with her on the porch of Prospect House.

"Do we look OK this time, Phyllis?" Annie asked, half-joking, half-seriously.

"Pretty good. Can I talk to you and not have it get back until my written report, Annie?"

"Sure."

"Well, I wish you fed them better. And I'm not sure the special-ed people over in the Department of Education think your teaching staff knows as much as they should about learning disabilities. And no one on staff has yet gotten the anger management training we recommended last year."

But Annie was struck at what she hadn't mentioned. "What about the staffing changes?"

"What staffing changes?"

And Annie suddenly knew she had just made a big mistake, mentioning the staff cuts before they were formally announced to the state.

"There's nothing about staffing changes in the progress report we received." Phyllis was sharp, and Annie knew she wouldn't let the issue go. Then Phyllis snapped her fingers and said "I just figured it out."

"Figured what out?"

"Figured out why our department's legislative person asked me the other day why The Houses had hired a lobbyist."

"A lobbyist? We don't have a lobbyist."

"No, but a big, quiet company that is talking about buying The Houses does. And their lobbyist has been writing legislation and slipping it to legislators they own—or could rent—to reduce the required staffing ratios for places like The Houses."

And then Annie saw the pieces, too. The new buyers were going to change the law and then announce the staffing cuts, and it would all be legal.

Phyllis went on. "We've heard reports that a major lobbying effort is under way to cut the staffing ratios so that these programs can make even more money. We started looking into it, and found a financial trail that leads to some very unusual new players in this area." She paused and looked around the porch to see if any of the windows were open. "Ever hear of a company called Blackoceans?"

"No." Annie was totally puzzled now, wondering where Phyllis was going and why she was telling her about it.

"They're a private contractor to the Defense Department. They run a lot of prisons and security operations in Iraq and places like that."

"Yeah. Now I remember. They got in trouble for shooting some civilians, didn't they?"

"Yeah. Someone apparently decided they were in so much trouble over there maybe it would be better and just as profitable if they ran prisons back here—only call them youth facilities. Set up a national franchise for youth detention programs."

"McLockup?"

"Something like that. This is a big business, Annie. You figure it out—you get twelve to fifteen thousand dollars a month for each girl, maybe more. You put up some cheap houses, you feed them generic cornflakes and watered-down fruit juice, you hire minimum wage watchers who come with their own hang-ups. Forgive me—I don't include you in that category. And you can make a ton of money doing it."

"How much money?"

"That's the thing—no one knows. The books are all proprietary—that's why they're converting the nonprofits to forprofits, so the expenses and revenues all become confidential." She looked at Annie, and reached over and patted her hand. "You watch out, Annie. These guys play for keeps. I'm telling you about this so you can keep an eye out for them."

Annie asked "But what does that say about the kinds of people who run these programs?"

Phyllis shook her head. "There are a dozen different types that run these programs, Annie—there's no one type. There are true believer clinical fanatics who believe they've invented the ultimate cure, the perfect therapy. There are religious fundies who want to pray away the kids' problems. And now there are corporate types who've figured out that you can make tons of money when you charge fifteen thousand a month and feed them Kool-Aid and cereal."

She paused, and then her voice softened. "And there are some saints—funny to talk about saints out here where they sing about them all the time—but there are real saints whose life work is doing all they can to ease the burden of these sad girls and their families. And you have to be very careful when you are digging out the bastards not to overlook the saints.

"Some of the best, hardest-working, and most caring professionals I have ever met in forty years of doing this work are in places like this. People like you, Annie, and people like the McAllisters over in Rose

House. These may be isolated and out of the way places, but good people come to places like this every day and work their butts off. And nothing the crummy staff do should ever obscure how hard some of these people work to save these girls' lives. And how important that work is."

Her eyes narrowed, and she picked up her clipboard. "And when I hear about how some new corporate wolves have come down out of the hills to try to squeeze more money out of these places, it makes me want to go back to my office and nail their hides to my wall!"

Annie rose as Phyllis stood up and began walking toward her car. "Thanks, Phyllis. I'll keep my eyes open."

Email
From: Annie Salinas to Geraldine Salinas
Subject: The BO Boys

Hey, Gerry.

Have you ever heard of Blackoceans? They do a lot of military contracting and now they want to run treatment programs like ours. We don't like what we've been hearing about them—lots of staff cuts may be coming up—save some room on your couch for me!

You and Mom used to say that I put too much of our worry about Irene into my work, and I've been thinking lately you may be right. Sometimes every girl who doesn't make it becomes another Irene to me—and it just breaks my heart. But when these new guys come in and take over the program and start trying to figure out ways to save money on these girls—it makes me furious.

More later,

Love you,
Annie

37

Lexie

One of the things I hated most about the program was all the stupid writing we had to do. Whoever came up with the program apparently thought that we could all cure ourselves by writing stupid essays about our lives. There was this long list of "topics" that somebody had made up years ago, and copies of the topics were handed out as punishments. I never understood it—we were supposed to be learning by doing the writing, but the writing was given out as a punishment or to get points—not as a learning exercise. It made no sense.

The topics were things like "What reflections do you have about the incident that caused this problem?" "What thinking errors led to the problem?" "What I will do differently next time to avoid this problem?" "What are my coping strategies when I feel stressed?" Same questions, over and over.

After a while we got to where we could just pump out these dopey paragraphs that would get them off our case. It was one more part of the phony stuff we had to do to get through the program. Everyone learned to write really big, and slowly, so that a half hour would go by and we would have written one or two paragraphs at most.

There were some phrases that we learned to use over and over—stuff that the staff liked to read that somehow convinced them we were making progress:

I've been thinking a lot about . . .
Lately I've realized . . .

I know I haven't always thought clearly before I acted.
I really want to do better at . . .
When I get back home I want to work hard at . . .

Annie made us do the writing crap sometimes, but you could tell that she didn't think it was as important as the rest of the staff did. Annie would rather push you to give her good answers to hard questions than to have you write some BS you didn't really believe.

Annie and I had kept running, and we tried to get out at least once a week. She would stick her head in the room after my last class on Friday, and ask me if I wanted to go for a run. We had worked out a path that went up into the hills and then circled down across some of the horse ranches behind The Houses. It was a good four mile run, and we had both gotten to where we could do it at an eight-minute pace and keep talking along the way. The weather had stayed cold, but once we got going, we warmed up right away and the path was usually clear of the snow that covered the higher foothills.

Running was helping, and it reminded me how running had worked for me at home. It was funny, kind of. They talk here about your "coping strategies," which meant whatever helped you calm down when you got angry or frustrated. Running here in the hills was different from running at home along the river by our house, but it worked here to quiet me down, the same way it did at home.

So I ran so I wouldn't run. And running with Annie had helped me realize that I could just keep doing that at home when things got to be too much for me in the house. It was a coping strategy that really helped me cope.

Once a month an "outside speaker" came in to talk to us about something the program staff thought was important. It was usually the same old stuff—drugs are bad, drugs we prescribe are good, parents are people too—all of it kind of "duh" stuff.

This month's speaker was supposed to be talking to us about "girls around the world." No one could figure out what that meant, so we were a little more interested than usual. Mostly the titles sounded like someone preaching at us.

But this lady turned out to be anything but a preacher. Her name was Dorothy Beecher—she called herself Dot.

She came into the family room after dinner and began setting up a PowerPoint presentation. By now we had all seen lots of them, mostly boring ones with people reading each slide line by line, as if they thought we were either blind or too stupid to understand the big words. She explained her work, and it turned out she was from some organization called Doctors without Borders. They give medical care to people in other countries—poor countries, mostly. She talked about how bad the health conditions are in those places and showed some gross pictures of kids with all kinds of diseases. She talked a lot about the girls in these countries and how their culture meant that most of them couldn't go to school and had to marry somebody chosen by their parents when they were as young as 7 or 8. She showed us a book called *Half the Sky* that was all about girls and women and how bad things were for many of them.

When she finished the slide show, she stopped and just looked at us. Just when it was getting uncomfortable, she started talking again. She had an angry look on her face.

"Most of you kids are mall rats, and a few of you aren't. But every last one of you is better off than the girls I've been talking about. You know where your next meal is coming from, you know where you're sleeping tonight, and you won't have to do some creepy thing for some creepy guy to get a place to stay. You're safe—in a way none of these girls is safe.

"So you want my wrap-up message? Here it is—short and sweet. Number 1—stop feeling sorry for yourselves. Number 2—go home and do what you need to do to stay out of places like this. And number 3—for God's sake, spend part of the rest of your life thinking about somebody besides yourself and remember all those other girls out there and how much help you could give them."

She paused and then softened her voice, almost pleading with us. "Each one of you, without a doubt, could do something to change the lives of one of these girls. I am positive about that. With a check, with a letter, with a book, or by someday spending time out there or around the corner in your own home town, teaching one of them to read—you could change their lives. And while you were doing it for them, you'd no longer be thinking just about yourself." She paused again, and then asked, "You want somebody to come change you?" She pointed at us, one by one. "Then go change somebody else's life and it may just happen to you at the same time. And, by the way, that's the message of every decent religion on the planet."

We all just sat there. No one had ever talked to us that way. I didn't know how the others felt, although I could tell by the way she was scowling that Belinda was really pissed. But I was just amazed that Dot Beecher had talked to us that way. We were always "the bad girls" or girls who needed to stop doing bad things. But what Dot had told us was that we didn't have it so bad compared to millions of other kids in the world.

She made me think a lot about being here, and I guess that was her point. And I got what she was saying about other girls in other places. Sure, a kid in a slum in India or living on the streets in Chicago is a lot worse off than we are here. Of course knowing that we'll get fed and that we're safe here is better than those kids have it.

But it doesn't make it feel any better to wake up here and know that you're a thousand miles from your home and your family and friends.

And she's right, I guess, that most of us are pretty wrapped up in ourselves most of the time. Although with staff walking around all the time saying "think about what you're going to do to turn your life around"—who else are you supposed to focus on? We're here because we screwed up or because we're screwed up—or both. That's about us, they keep telling us we're supposed to work on ourselves. Not some kid in India.

I looked around as the session was breaking up. I was sitting next to Laila, who had been staring at Dot since she began talking. It dawned on me that talking about girls in other countries must have really gotten to her. She had her head lowered, and I heard her crying, so softly that I don't think anyone else heard her. Her shoulders were barely moving, and I reached over to try to comfort her, and lightly patted her on the back. She jerked away, and then saw it was me, and tried to smile through her tears. And I got a tiny inkling of what Dot was talking about, and how close Laila must have been to a really awful life.

And so I did the only thing I could think of. I leaned over and whispered to her "I'm really glad you're here."

She didn't look at me, but she reached out and gave my hand a quick squeeze.

38

Annie

Annie was at the central office for another lecture. This one was about sexuality, and she supposed it would be some boring discussion of adolescent masturbation. It turned out to be a bit more.

The lecturer was a St Louis-based M.D., Lewis Ralston, who had worked with RTCs all over the country. He was in his late thirties, Annie thought, and was dressed informally in a sweater.

Ralston began. "As you all know, one of the trickiest parts of programs for girls is how you staff them, and how you handle sexuality. Adolescent girls in general are interested in sex, most of them, and to make it worse, some of the disorders we deal with have symptoms that manifest themselves in sexual terms. Add the ingredient that these girls are looking for any way they can to get out of here, and you've got a highly combustible mixture."

He went on to talk about some case histories, and Annie was horrified by some of his stories. He started the case histories by saying that he was deliberately balancing cases where girls had been victimized with cases where girls were trying to manipulate the system—because both problems were real.

"Staff at one of the places where we did consulting work told us that any time there was an incident of physical conflict among girls or between girls and staff, if male staff were involved, within seconds girls would take off their shirts and start tearing their clothes to manufacture 'evidence' of assault. Male staff began leaving the building when there was a problem, which led to arguments with female staff, and the whole program broke down after a while because they were all arguing about how to respond to the girls acting out—and not dealing with any of the causes of the acting out."

"There are also far too many sad cases where girls were definitely molested and sexually abused by male and female staff who somehow got through the screening. Some of these are called 'consenting cases,' but how a mentally ill 15 year-old consents to anything sexual is beyond me. But lawyers have to say something, I guess."

"In some programs, the solution has been putting cameras everywhere but in the bathrooms. Then a staff member has to be placed in charge of camera patrol, and then there are endless debates about how long to keep tapes, and everybody worries about what might happen if the camera shows other kinds of negligence by the agency—not just sexual shenanigans. Other programs have redoubled their efforts to screen staff for sexual abnormalities, using some fairly intrusive and expensive methods, including private investigators."

"Programs that have been publicly identified with sexual abuse—and there have been several of them—have had their admissions drop way off. More and more people are Googling these programs, and it only takes one news story or blog by an angry kid to turn off a prospective parent." He paused, and smiled. "Interestingly, the coed programs have had fewer problems than the single-sex programs, in general, because they worry about sex from day one in coed programs."

A hand went up from the back of the room. "What about homosexuality among the girls themselves?"

Ralston sighed. "For millennia, in every institution where we segregate by sex, some people will figure out how to have sex. They will always be a minority, some of the sex will be coercive, and some will be consensual. Adolescent girls are no different. Some of what goes on is simply an attempt to shock adults in a place where kids don't have many tools of power." Then his voice softened. "And some of it is genuine emotion by girls who are sexually different and who, like every single girl in these programs, sometimes just want to be comforted. Like most of us, they long for a gentle touch in the night."

A shocked voice came back. "But are you condoning it?"

He frowned. "No more than I condone punishing children for their symptoms. Look, let me try to sum up before I take more questions. You can't eliminate sexuality from programs involving adolescents. They are at the age where they are supposed to be fixated on sex. It's how their hard wiring works. But you can talk about it frankly, and set clear boundaries, and let girls—and boys—feel safe if they need to report something they don't like, whether it involves them or another person."

"And let's be clear here—what we are watching out for is addictions, not experiments. We all have our own addictions. Drugs, booze, nicotine, sex. Or the raw edge of risk—climbing rocks or mountains. Caffeine, fancy shoes, food—or no food, watching mindless TV shows, books, travel, new stuff for the house or for the kids, video games and new toys. And for some of us, it's work. We're addicted to the good parts and the numbing parts of work."

He paused, watching them. "We all want the blissful high—even if it's just the high you get from sitting doing nothing. And addictions get us closer to that high—or convince us that they do, so we'll keep going back to them."

"And the difference is that some of us can keep them under control and know where the edge of the cliff is. And others just don't. They have no idea where to stop or how to stop. And they all get stuck trying to cross that river in Egypt that every addict knows about: 'De Nile.'"

As Annie walked to her car to drive back to The Houses, she thought about the lecture. There had been an incident at The Houses three years ago, and both the male staffer, a classroom teacher, and the girl involved had been hustled off campus as swiftly as possible. But she wasn't at all sure that all the lessons that Ralston had talked about had been absorbed by the program. And she wondered what might be going on that none of the management knew about.

Annie and Greg had dated a few times, and Annie had decided that it was time for them to move on with the relationship. They had exchanged a few chaste little kisses after their dates, but Greg had been very proper with her, and Annie wondered what was going to happen next.

She liked Greg, she guessed, because he was good-looking, smart, and cared about the work that was still at the center of her life. But she had no idea where he was about sex. Annie thought of her sex life in college and the years after as par-level, with a few casual hookups, two serious relationships, and a lot of flirting that never went anywhere. Annie had figured out early on that she liked sex a lot, but had seen it really mess people up, like any addiction, and after some early mistakes on the casual side of sex, she was careful to keep it in proportion to the rest of a relationship.

Annie never thought of herself as promiscuous, but once during her college years her sister Bea had sat Annie down and given her what Annie called the "saffron lecture." Bea drew a line and made four marks on it, with the letters *S, F, R* and *N*. She told Annie they stood for safe, fun, risky, and nuts—the four stages of sex. She told Annie she needed to stay on the fun side of the fun-risky part of the spectrum. Annie never forgot the point.

Her cardinal principles had come to be that if the guy could make her laugh, was reasonably good-looking (which she defined as no worse than Will Farrell), didn't have stupid political ideas, and had clean fingernails, sex was at least possible. Those guidelines had kept her out of any serious physical connections during the five years since she had started working at The Houses.

She and Greg had fallen into a pattern of getting together after the lectures at the central office, having dinner, and then driving home to their separate apartments. This time Greg asked her to come back for coffee, and she accepted.

Greg's apartment was predictably that of a late-20's professional, mostly mid-range Ikea, with a few exceptions. He had a collection of prints on one wall, and some photographs of what looked like Western deserts. He explained that he had spent some time after graduate school hiking in a number of the deserts of the American West and Southwest, and the photos were all his own.

"What are these prints? Some of these look Mexican."

"They are. I collected a few when I was on a language semester down there in college. My mother used to run an art gallery, and she helped me choose them."

Annie went over to two of the prints, one of a group of three women and another of a pair of hands—both of which were strikingly spare with strong lines. "Who are these by?"

"José Clemente Orozco. Aren't they powerful? I love that one called La Familia. And this is by David Siquieros, and this one is a print of Diego Rivera's."

"Who knew you were a connoisseur of Mexican art?"

Greg walked over and put his arms around her. "Yes, but it's the living versions of great art that I like the most."

"Oh, you silver-tongued devil."

"Who, me?"

They went into his kitchen and he made some passable coffee—at least it wasn't instant, Annie thought as he hustled around getting cups and fussing with his coffeemaker. Coffee was never available at The Houses, and for Annie it was a rare treat to drink someone else's. They went back into the small living room and sat down.

"So what's happening at the Big HQ?" That was the phrase Annie used, somewhat teasingly, when she referred to the central office.

He frowned, then sipped his coffee. "I'm trying to figure out where to go next. They've started telling me I need to decide whether I want to do basic research on the program or keep doing the kind of mini-studies I have been doing. They say they can give me a promotion if I publish something about the program." He looked away from Annie at the prints on the wall. "They've sort of suggested that I should write about how successful the program is."

Annie knew what he wasn't saying. The top management wanted a positive report—whether the results were positive or not.

"So how do you feel about that? Sounds like it might not fit with your ideas about outcomes."

Greg smiled, somewhat sadly. "Good therapist question. I'm not sure."

Annie wondered if she could influence Greg's decision, and then she wondered if she should try to. *If he doesn't know what he's going to do, why should I try to push him one way or another?* But a parallel idea kept sliding into her thinking: *maybe I could win him over to the right side.* Her desire to influence him was getting mixed up with her desire to go to bed with him, and she finally decided to stop trying to sort them out—and just go to bed with him.

"I'm trying to decide where to go next, too. Why don't we try to decide in there?" she said, pointing to his bedroom.

Greg froze for a second, and then recovered. "Great idea. You sure? No, forget I asked that," he said as he saw Annie's eyebrow rise. "Come on," and he stood up, took her hand and led her into the bedroom.

After a strenuous and fairly loud hour or so, they lay together on the bed, semi-spooning. Greg had his arm around Annie's waist and was nestled into her neck. He quietly asked "Am I allowed to say thank you?"

"If I can say the same."

So together they said "Thank you." And Annie added, knowing how much reassurance most men in their twenties needed, "That was great."

"Good. I mean great."

Driving home, Annie caught her lingering smile in her rear view mirror and said to herself, *you needed that, girl. But take it easy. The boy hasn't yet decided who he is.*

Email
From: Annie Salinas to Beatrice Salinas
Subject: Sex lectures and clinical work

    Hey, Bea. Little bit of news here. I've told you we go to these lectures over at our headquarters office in Desert City, which are sometimes good and sometimes dry as dust. This week we had a good one on sexuality in residential programs. (And before you email me back and say it's about time I got some sex education—keep it to yourself!) It made a lot of sense, even though some of the old fogies thought the lecturer was encouraging practices that were too "tolerant."

    I've mentioned this guy that I met a few months ago who works in the central office of The Houses program. Without going into the details, we had a fine night together after the lecture. No idea where it's going (now I hear you saying "loose woman"). I'm not sure he's a real grownup yet, but it was fun (F on the saffron scale) and he's good company. For now.

Love you,
Annie

39

Lexie

Sheila had come to me in class and whispered that she had something to show me. I invented an excuse to go back by the computers and sat down quietly next to her. She touched a key and I saw a balance sheet, just like a thousand balance sheets and income statements I had seen spread out over my dad's worktable at home. I remembered a few things my dad had tried to show me, and began to make sense of the tables.

"OK, this is an income statement, here's revenues, here's spending, and this should be annual profits. Wow. Looks like 45% profit, if these numbers are right."

"But look, Lexie." She pushed another key, and a second balance sheet popped up. Only this one was fancier, and was a page from a book that I recognized as the annual report of The Houses that was on the front table in the entry way. And when I looked at, it showed no profit—the revenues and spending balanced out exactly.

Sheila put into words what I had just figured out. "They have two sets of books, Lexie! This is from their annual report—and the other one—the one that shows a 45% profit—is the projection for next year. And there's something else—the name of the company changes. It's all The Houses in the annual report and then next year it changes to BO." She giggled. "Body odor?!"

"Must be a new owner or something," I said.

Then she got very intense, looking up at the teacher and around the classroom. "I just printed it out in the empty classroom in Prospect.

There's a printer in the closet there and I wired it to print from here. So get the printout when you go back to Prospect. And don't let anyone catch you with it. This is so explosive, Lexie. If they knew we had it—I don't know what they'd do. It's much worse than what we thought."

"Yeah." I remembered something else my dad had said when we were talking about what he called "forensic accounting." He was trying to make his job seem more interesting, and he told me about some of the great corporate rip-offs of recent years. But one thing he said was popping up right now.

"Sheila, it's a federal crime to have two sets of books if you're using federal money. They'd go crazy if they knew we had this. Shut it down, Sheila, right away."

Now we were both scared. I started watching the clock, waiting for the period to end so I could race back to Prospect and get the printout.

40

Annie

Annie was in the staff office when the front door burst open and someone came running down the hall. She stepped out and spotted Lexie racing into the classroom area.

"Whoa, whoa!" she yelled at Lexie, who almost fell down trying to stop her forward momentum. "Why are you running?"

But Lexie was breathing so hard she couldn't talk yet. "Uh, uh," she gasped.

"Take your time," Annie said.

"Uh, uh—I wanted to see if I left my book in here."

"No, try again, and if you lie to me again, Lexie, I'll know it."

Annie could see that Lexie was now in anguish, wanting to get whatever she had started into the classroom to retrieve, and not wanting Annie to know about it. She assumed it was some kind of contraband, which made her sad, because she thought Lexie was making progress. Lexie was looking at her, trying to make a decision. Annie remained quiet, hoping it was the right one.

"I need to trust you with something, Annie." Lexie spoke very quietly, still trying to catch her breath, watching Annie's face for a sign of something she couldn't put into words. "I know how hard you work and how much you care about all the girls. But I need to trust you."

"Come into the office and tell me about it."

So she did. She explained to Annie what Sheila had done. She didn't use her name, but Annie knew Sheila was the only computer genius in The Houses, and she didn't need Lexie to tell her who had done it. Lexie told Annie that they had discovered some very damaging evidence that the managers of The Houses—she couldn't tell if it was the old ones or the new ones yet—were using fake financial reports to hide the profits they were planning to take out of the program.

And more of the pieces fell into place for Annie. Why the new owners were trying to change the state laws, and why Suzanne had been so nervous about Greg's questions and her research on what happened to the girls after they left The Houses. Lexie and Sheila had found one of the missing pieces, and the only question that remained was what Annie was going to do about it.

"You did right to tell me, Lexie. I won't ask how you got this—but I think I know. Don't worry, I'll protect you guys."

But Annie couldn't stop to focus on the Blackoceans discovery yet, because she was five minutes late for a therapy session. Annie had worried about Laila after the Dot Beecher lecture. She had seen how she reacted at the time, and Laila had stayed almost completely shut down since then. And so Annie scheduled a session with her.

Laila had been as uncommunicative as usual in a group session, and Annie asked her to stay after the group had filed out of the room. When the door closed and the two of them were left, Annie said, as gently as she could, "Laila, I'm trying to help you, but I can't do it unless I know more about what you need. Can you tell me anything that will help me?"

Laila looked at her, drew a deep breath, and nodded. Then she said "I will tell you once, and then I never want to talk to you or anyone else about it again. All right?"

"Yes."

She shook, her fists clenched, trying to gather the strength to speak. Then she leaned forward and whispered to Annie, "I was sold when I was seven. My parents sold me." Then she froze, lowering her head and sitting so still that Annie thought she had passed out until she saw her breathing.

All Annie could say was "I am so sorry, Laila." She paused, uncertain whether to press ahead. Then she added, "I just want to say one thing, and then we won't mention it again. Remember that movie we saw a few weeks ago, *Good Will Hunting*? Do you remember what Robin Williams kept saying to the young man, over and over? 'It's not your fault. *It's not your fault.*'"

She started to pat Laila, and then pulled her hand back. "I totally understand why you don't want to talk about it. We won't mention it again."

Annie knew she had been right to try to reach Laila. But it made her feel as helpless as she had ever been since starting work at The Houses. With one horrifying word, *sold*, Laila forced Annie to admit there were some outrages that were so far beyond therapy or medications that she had no idea what to do—except to make sure a girl was safe and sheltered for the moment.

41

Lexie

After talking to Annie, I was still scared, but I knew I had told the one person at The Houses who might be able to help us. Annie took the only copy of the printout after promising me she wouldn't do anything with it without telling us.

I told my dad on the phone that night that I needed to talk to him about something, and right away he asked me if I wanted him to come see me. I liked it that he would drop everything and come try to help. I told him not yet, that I was talking to a staff member that I trusted and that I needed to go over it with her again. I explained what we had found, but I didn't tell him how we got it—and he didn't ask.

And I told him that something he had showed me about his accounting work had helped me a lot. I knew he would like that, and he did. We had hardly ever talked about his work, because I had been too wrapped up in my own stuff to care, and his work seemed really boring to me. But now I saw a little glimmer of how his work could really help people, and I told him he had really helped me. His work had really helped me.

I thought I heard him crying for a moment, but maybe I was mistaken.

Later that night I talked to Sheila, who was still freaked out. I tried to calm her down, and then I got an idea.

"Sheila, can you get into their email?"

"You mean central office?

"Yeah."

"Sure I can. But that's even riskier than hacking their financials. What if Annie tells them and they put up some kind of super firewall that can trace me?"

"Annie isn't going to tell anybody. What if you just searched for anything that mentions Prospect House to see if they are onto us?"

"Yeah." She thought about it for a minute. "There's a kind of superfast search that can get in and out without any trace. At least if they are using normal software. But what if they use the firewall tools that the military uses?"

"Yeah. Maybe it's too risky." I could see that Sheila was torn between conquering a new cyber-barrier and worrying about getting caught. Her cockiness finally won out. "OK, I'll do it. Tomorrow morning, in and out fast."

The next day I tried not to watch her in the back of the room. Within five minutes, she came up and sat in the seat next to me on the window side of the classroom. She whispered. "Got it. Looks like they're snooping around but don't have anything yet."

But two days later, the doorbell rang. When Annie opened it, there was a huge block of a human standing there, crew-cut, with muscles on his muscles. He handed Annie a folder. I was watching from around the corner in the family room.

"I have a request from the central office to look at your computers and do some fingerprinting." He showed Annie a folder with some paper in it. She could see that it had The Houses letterhead at the top.

Annie said, "I don't think so. Who should I call in the central office to check this authorization? And what is your name, please?"

And then Belinda walked up to him with Dolores, the next biggest one of us, who had about six tattoos. Dolores said, "You got a problem with us using computers, big man?" And Belinda just glared at him.

Then Laurie, all five feet one inch of her, walked up to this huge guy and said "What's your name, rank, and serial number, trooper? You look like the kind of guy who washes out of Special Forces and then has to go to work for a scumbag contractor. I've got the phone number for the IG in DoD—you want to get reported?" She reached for a pen and pad from the table in the hallway and stood waiting for his response.

Laurie's father was ex-military and sometimes she'd use military slang.

It was a bluff. But sometimes people thought we were such freaks and delinquents that they gave us powers we didn't even have. But this guy didn't know that.

Then Annie rejoined the conversation. "Laurie has a point. I'd like your identification, please, and the name of your superior so I can check out your authorization to review our computers. Each of these girls has privacy rights endorsed by the state government, and I'd like to know your basis for reviewing information about them."

The guy looked totally confused by this time. Laurie was still standing there with her pad of paper, glaring at the guy. He looked at Laurie, looked at Annie, and made his decision.

"Bunch of little girls." He said disgustedly. "They don't pay me enough for this BS." And he got in his car, put on his dark glasses, and drove away.

Annie called us all into the kitchen, and sat us down around the big table. "What was that all about?"

Laurie spoke up, cocky with the victory. "Dude wanted to harass us. We backed him down. Then he left."

Annie shook her head, smiling. "Sometimes you guys amaze me." She just looked at us for a while. "Do you realize how powerful you are when you stand together?"

No one answered, but there were a lot of smiles and a snicker or two. Annie said, "All right, get out of here and get ready for dinner."

Two days later, I was in the kitchen when Belinda came in and whispered to me "They're going to kick Sophia out. I just heard it from Laurie who overheard a phone call over in main building. They're sending her home."

"Dammit. She's got nothing going at home. She lives with her aunt and it's totally Druggie City. That is so wrong."

I went to Annie's office as soon as I could, and asked her why they were kicking Sophia out. Annie frowned and said "Sophia said she is just going to keep exploding and attacking staff until they send her home. So central office has decided we can't keep her any longer."

"But it isn't Sophia who is starting the explosions! They set her off—you said it yourself. Can't you get them to give her one more chance?" Annie kept motioning for me to sit down, but I was too angry to sit.

"I told you to forget that conversation, Lexie. I tried as hard as I could, I can't tell you what I did, but I tried as hard as I could to get them to keep her. But I lost. She has to go home."

"That is so unfair. This place really sucks." I knew it wasn't Annie's fault, but just then I was mad at all of them.

Upstairs in the bathroom, I found another one of Laila's haiku that said some of what I was feeling:

These dirty brown hills
Squat there, watching us watch them.
They're prisoners too.

42

Annie

Annie met with Suzanne in the staff office at Prospect. Annie had called her and told her that she needed to talk with her urgently.

Suzanne had made clear on the call that she wasn't going to talk any more about Sophia. Annie had used every argument she could think of to try to get a reversal of the senior staff's decision to terminate Sophia. But Suzanne and the rest of them weren't budging. And Annie knew that there was little in Sophia's record to justify a hope that she would finally turn things around. Her M.O in her last two placements had been the same—coast along as far as she could and then turn to enough violence or non-compliance to make them boot her out. Annie knew from Sophia's file and the little bit of opening up she had done in therapy that they were sending Sophia back to a really hopeless situation, but she had no arguments left after the last explosion. So Annie reluctantly agreed with Suzanne that the conversation would not be about Sophia.

Annie had done some research of her own on the history of The Houses. The founders of The Houses were a very religious couple. Jake Stockmann had been the successful owner of a chain of hardware stores, and had expanded his business from California to Texas and Wyoming, eventually covering much of the inland West. By the time he retired he was worth several hundred million. He had founded The Houses and three other programs in other states. He and his wife Martha had visited The Houses two or three times a year, always coming out at Christmas with gifts for the girls.

But when Jake and Martha died, it turned out that none of their four children had ever acquired either the religious or charitable convictions of their parents. All four avoided having anything to do with the operation of the Houses. With some reverses to their portfolio, Annie began to see that the prospects of selling the residential programs could look very attractive to the Stockmann heirs. Annie had heard from Suzanne that one of the children convinced the others to invest in off-shore drilling just before the California platform blowouts off Santa Barbara had led to a five-year moratorium on off-shore projects.

Annie carefully explained that she had gotten some information about the new owners that looked very incriminating. When Suzanne asked where the information came from, Annie said "I can't tell you. It comes from someone I know outside the program who works in investments." She went on to go over each of the cuts and the "economies" that had weakened the program. She also described the new cuts she had learned about, and when she saw Suzanne reacting with little surprise, she realized how much Suzanne already knew.

Annie had called her father the night before to go over how she should play the meeting. She was glad she had called him. His advice was very simple: "Tell her the truth about what you know, tell her she has to change it, and tell her you're getting the hell out of there if it doesn't turn around."

Annie looked at Suzanne. "Suzanne, I know you've tried to make things work better here. We haven't always agreed, but I respect how hard you work and how much you care about the girls. But I can't let this happen. I won't let it happen to these girls. I need you to assure me that somebody in control will turn this around. The food, the staffing, the therapy cuts—all of it. If not, I will quit and do everything I can to take the program to state and federal agencies that will come in and do a total program audit."

Suzanne sat for a long time, looking down at her lap. Then she raised her head, and Annie could see that she had completely dropped her defenses. "Annie, you are asking every single question that I have asked for the last ten years. I know what we are doing wrong, and I know how to fix it. And I've made every one of these suggestions, and got shot down. Since Jake Stockmann died, this place has been on automatic pilot, and the only rule is don't spend money. They won't spend the money for good training. Or for the screening we need to weed out the staff that don't want to be here, the ones who will never understand these girls. All it would take is a little staff development, and an annual appraisal that was serious. I've suggested over and over that they ask the girls to rate the staff, the way any decent university today asks its students what they think of the faculty.

"When the new people came in, for a few weeks I believed they really were going to make it better. But now there's no doubt in my mind that they're going to make it worse. And right now I am the only thing standing between them and a much worse program. And I don't know what to do about it."

Annie said "Maybe you're not the only thing. But first we need to protect these girls. I think some of them are close to being ready to go home."

Suzanne nodded and said, "I agree, we should start focusing on that as soon as we can." She reached into her briefcase and pulled out a report that was several pages long. "Take a minute and look at what they are proposing now. I got this from someone at headquarters who is on our side but can't go public yet."

Annie skimmed the document quickly. It was an internal report from one Blackoceans executive to the CFO of the company. As she read, Annie saw that they not only wanted to change the staffing ratios—they wanted to change the staff. The memos were written in corporatese, but the intent was clear to Annie: save money and to hell with the girls.

We have found in our other sites and in researching other facilities that
residential staff do not have to hold master's degrees, Day treatment staff
who have the most direct contact with clients have been employed in many

other programs with high school degrees and even GEDs, and have worked out quite satisfactorily. When difficulties happen, warnings are issued and staff are terminated after a second incident. Turnover is always quite high in these positions, which keeps the pay rate low.

We have had considerable success in some of our facilities in the use of psychotropic medications to calm these clients down. Many of them tend toward violence and frequent emotional outbursts, which can cost considerable staff time and runs the risk of legal action. Using antidepressants in somewhat larger dosage has shown that a far more docile client is much less expensive to monitor.

We have also determined that additional operating costs can be saved by reducing therapy sessions and by using newly graduated MSWs to provide these services rather than experienced clinicians, who are considerably higher-salaried. We also recommend changing these therapy sessions from weekly to biweekly or even monthly for clients who appear to be making progress.

Since state and county agencies and schools pay a flat fee, any savings from these reductions in our costs go directly to our bottom line profits. When we are audited for cost baselines, we can use temporary staff hired with advanced degrees as the basis for the audit, and costs will appear higher than our actuals.

As Annie read it, she got a mental chill. It was so cold-blooded, with nothing about the girls or the program or anything beyond the profit potential of The Houses. She looked at Suzanne, handing the memo back. "It's worse than I thought. If you agree, I think we need to talk with some of the other staff who would be on our side." Suzanne nodded, and they began making their own plans.

That afternoon, Annie placed a call to Lexie's parents. "It looks like she's making a lot of progress, and we'd like to talk with you about her coming home. There's a lot happening here, as she may have told you, and I've talked with Suzanne, and she agrees Lexie and a few of the other girls are ready to begin transition planning."

They talked some more and Lexie's father said he wanted to come visit and talk with the senior managers about Lexie and the program changes. Annie said she would tell Suzanne and they would set up a time to meet.

The next morning, Lexie's father arrived from California and immediately asked for a meeting with Suzanne. Two other pairs of parents were visiting and Suzanne had suggested they all meet informally to go over any concerns they had at the end of the visits. Annie had been asked to sit in on the visit because all of the parents had girls in Prospect.

Suzanne began by asking the parents if they had any questions. Lexie's father pulled some notes out of his coat pocket, and looked down at them. Then he gave Suzanne an angry glance. "I'm an auditor, so I read the GAO's audit reports from time to time. Some of them are pretty painful to read. Maybe we agree Lexie is ready to leave, but I can't just pack her up and leave without trying to clear up some things I've come across. I'm not sure what they have to do with the new owners you told us about a while ago, but they really are a problem for me." He paused, and looked at some notes he had pulled from his coat.

"The federal government has completely failed to keep an eye on these residential programs, despite hundreds of millions of federal dollars flowing to them. Over 250,000 children and youth were in some kind of residential program in 2005. Three different federal agencies have responsibility for these kids, but there is no overall report on problems compiled anywhere in the federal government. The 2008 GAO report to George Miller's congressional committee is horrifying, because it talks about specific kids who died due to mistreatment or negligence. In 2005 GAO found there were over 1,500 reports on abuse in residential programs—and they said the number was definitely understated because of bad reporting.

"In January 2009, the National Disability Rights Network issued a report documenting dozens of instances where students with disabilities were pinned to the floor for hours at a time, handcuffed, locked in closets, and subjected to what GAO called 'other traumatizing acts of violence.' These are not delinquents—these are kids with disabilities who did something a staff member didn't like—and some of them were only 5 or 6 years old!

"The GAO report said that untrained staff, lack of adequate nourishment—some kids were starved as discipline—and 'reckless or negligent operating practices' were widespread."

He stopped and looked at Suzanne. "So what does the national organization that represents these programs say? The association that your agency belongs to does not investigate any allegations of wrongdoing and rarely sanctions any of its members."

Again, he paused and looked at Suzanne for several moments without saying anything. She would not return his steady gaze, but shook her head as if she disagreed. Finally he spoke again. "What does your agency have to say about this? What is your position on the congressional legislation that was passed in 2008? I am not saying that this program is guilty, but you belong to the national organization that ignored the problems. Correct?"

Suzanne motioned dismissively with her hands. "You're quite right that we had nothing to do with the incidents in the GAO report. We support the reform legislation that recently passed, and we support its intent. And we have written our national organization and urged them to comply with the legislation in every respect. Now, can we get on with the meeting?"

The rest of the parents sat saying nothing. Finally, one of the mothers said "I had no idea the problems were this bad in other programs. Are you sure you've done everything you can to make sure nothing like this ever happens here?"

"Yes." But before she could say anything else, Lexie's father spoke up and asked another question, with far more anger in his voice than he had shown in his recital of the facts of the GAO report.

"Then why is this agency lobbying the state legislature to reduce the staffing ratio in this program? You know that inadequate staffing was one of the reasons cited by the GAO report as a cause of the problems. So why try to make it worse?"

Suzanne looked like she had been slapped. She answered weakly, "That was a decision made in our central office. I had nothing to do with it."

Ted Crockett answered her immediately. "If this isn't being handled at your level, I'm going to have to write the other parents and set up a session in the central office."

Suzanne looked at him and said quietly "That would be a good idea, Mr. Crockett."

A week later, the regular quarterly parents' meeting was held.

Annie took her seat in the quarterly parents' meeting for Prospect, which was being held in the conference room in the classroom building. Five sets of parents had arrived, and Annie quickly saw that once again, the missing parents tended to be those of the girls who were having the worst problems. Monica's parents, Dolores', Lexie's father, Holly's mother, and Laurie's mother were arranging themselves around the conference table, and Suzanne had come in to take her place at the head of the table. No one was talking very much, in contrast with the chattiness of the session three months before.

As the parents gathered in the meeting room of the education building, Annie noticed a whispered side conversation between Monica's father, Frank Millstein, and Ted Crockett.

Suzanne began by inviting the parents to "share how you are feeling about your girls' progress."

Frank Millstein took control right away. "The last time we met, you mentioned new owners. That was three months ago. But we have no new information since then. I have to tell you my wife and I have had serious discussions about pulling our daughter out of the program."

One of the mothers leaned forward and said "You have?"

"Yes. We're concerned about not knowing where the new owners are going or even knowing who they are. We researched this place very carefully on the internet before sending Monica here, and now it looks as if some major changes are being made, and we aren't being told what they are."

Suzanne started to speak, and then sat back as she saw Ted Crockett pulling out a file out of his large briefcase. "I've done some investigation on recent securities filings and it looks like the new owners are a company called Blackoceans. They've worked in the military contracting field in the past and seem to now be switching to domestic programs. Frankly, this does not seem like the kind of firm that would have any clue how to deal with 15 year-old girls with mental and emotional problems."

Annie had read somewhere about forensic accounting and she assumed that Ted Crockett was familiar with the field.

Ted continued. "We asked for a meeting with the Blackoceans central office but they kept referring us back to you. When we told them you didn't know anything, they said you were being briefed and would know more very soon. It's a classic run-around, but we're not going to get anywhere with them without legal action. Or without pulling our girls out. And that's where I am. So you feel free to tell them that a group of parents will be pulling our girls out."

Suzanne looked even sadder, and shook her head. She said "Frankly, I'm not sure that will affect them. There are so many school districts and state and local mental health agencies that will send girls to bad programs, sub-standard programs, just to get them out of their schools, that they would fill those beds within a week. That's the sad truth."

Annie said, "I don't know much about the changes you've asked about. Suzanne is more current on those than I am, but neither of us knows for sure what will happen. So what I'm saying is more about what you'll be facing whether your girls are here or home or somewhere else. But I do know this: those of you who are here made a great effort to be here, and to work with us on the program. And your girls need you to continue to make that effort."

Ted Crockett said, with a frown, "I appreciate everything you're saying, but it seems as if the two of you are not really involved in the decision-making about what happens next. Am I right?"

It was hard for Suzanne to answer, Annie could see, but she finally did. "You're right. We've only been briefed on a few of the changes—as you and I discussed last week, Mr. Crockett."

Monica's father said, "Then how soon do you think we are going to find out more? And should a group of us get in touch with the new owners directly?"

Suzanne quickly answered, "That's exactly what I would do if I were in your place."

Annie called Greg after the meeting. "I need to talk to you, right away. I'm coming over to your place after work."

Annie burst in the front door. Greg was sitting on the couch, and did not get up. "Greg, they're definitely going to sell the company to some corporate jerks who are going to fire some of the staff to make more money! The parents know all about it."

"I know, I just heard."

"You just heard—when?" Annie was suddenly certain that Greg had known about the sale earlier but had not told her.

"They told us last week."

"And you didn't tell me? Thanks for nothing."

"Annie, I knew you would be upset, and I wanted to find out more about what was happening."

"You knew I would be upset so you wouldn't tell me? How does that make sense?" Then she stopped. "They offered you the promotion, didn't they?" He was silent. "Didn't they?!"

"Yes." He still would not look at her.

"Oh, Greg, they bought you off. You poor little kid—they bought you off. Don't you know that's how people start to corrupt themselves—they get bought off with a job or a promotion or some kind of pathetic spotlight that they need." She stopped, saddened, watching him. "Greg, no one can corrupt you if you don't want to be."

"Annie, we're not all crusaders. You want to call me a kid and tell me I'm corrupt, fine." He was furious, and jabbed his finger at her, still refusing to stand up. "But you're the immature one who thinks you can quit this job and just go on to another one. This is how it works, Annie. And you're leaving those girls behind—if you think these guys are bad for the company, why are you leaving those girls behind?"

"So do something about it, Greg! You said you were going to do something with the work I did on outcomes for the girls who've gone through Prospect. You said that was a big deal, that I'd found something important."

"I can't touch that right now. It's too explosive." He looked angry, and embarrassed, all at once. And Annie knew that he was overdrawn on whatever emotional resources he used in making decisions about his life.

Greg then said, "It's like all that beer in the fridge that you've been allowing yourself to drink so carefully. You can't control everything, Annie, no matter how much you want to and need to."

"No, I can't. But I can damn well control who I trust. And you just dropped off that list, bud."

She shook her head, disgusted now. "How dare you talk to me about what those girls need? These girls—these precious girls. All the violence they endured and the alcohol and drugs their parents did and the bad luck of their genes. But they keep on, most of them. Despite all the wreckage they've come through, they try to get it right, they try to become like the rest of the girls back home, the lucky ones, the ones they call the Barbies, the normies. And the best of them will be all right. They'll sort it out and climb impossibly high mountains the rest of us couldn't even dream of facing. They deserve so much more than they're getting from these places, and yet they'll have to make their own way, most of the time, on their own, inventing a life better than the one they got from their parents and their so-called government."

She paused, trying to keep under control, furious that he could not see it. She shook her fist at him, speechless, then finally saying in a much quieter voice, "And I will do anything I can for them, for my sister, for all of them. Anything."

She grabbed her coat from the couch. "I think we're done here, don't you?"

"I guess so. I'm sorry you're reacting this way."

"And I'm sorry you didn't draw the line you should have." And she reached down and stroked his face. "Call me if you change your mind."

As she walked to her car, she was mostly glad that she hadn't added the final phrase that she'd started to say—or if you find your *cojones*. He wasn't going to change.

Email
From: Annie Salinas to Beatrice Salinas
Subject: Boys and buses otra vez

Hey, Bea.

Remember the guy I told you about a while ago? And I wasn't sure he was a grownup yet? Well, it turns out my emotional immaturity detector is still working—he crapped out on some stuff at work where he needed to stand up and be tough—and instead he took a promotion and backed down.

Disappointing as hell. Where are all the tough guys, huh? He said I was asking him to live up to too high a standard, and I told him he was corrupt. A real scumbag company has bought our company out and it looks like they're making a lot of changes—none of them good. And this guy is going along with them.

So looks like we may not have any more strenuous evenings together. Oh, well. Remember what Mama always said: boys are like buses—always another one coming along.

Love you,
Annie

43

Lexie

The doorbell rang, and it was my dad. I had no idea he was coming, and first I got my hopes up that he was going to take me away. And then I got all worried that he was here because they were going to do something to me for getting involved with Sheila's hacking. Then I worried about my mom.

I hugged him and after Sue signed him in we went into the fancy room. He looked very serious, even angry. "What's the matter, Dad? What's happened? Is Mom OK?"

"Your mother is fine. She wanted to come but we decided I needed to meet with the people running the program." He took off his coat and tossed it on the couch. "Lexie, we know you've been trying to work the program here and make progress. You've told us how much you like Annie, and how much she's helped you think about the choices you need to make. That's all good, and that makes us wish you could stay here." He saw me start to smile at the thought of getting home, and he quickly added, "But we aren't considering taking you out of here because your treatment is complete. It's because we've learned some things about this program—partly from the information you and the other girl gave me—that makes us sure this is not the right place for you."

"So I'm leaving? Are you going to stick me in some other program—is that why you're here?" I was getting angry, having the idea of going home held out and then taken away.

"Lexie, it's up to you. We told you when you started to get into trouble with the running away and ditching and wrecking things in the house that we were going to lose control over what happened to you. You kept blaming us, and doing whatever you wanted—and this is where it got you." Then he got a very sad look on his face, almost like he was going to cry. "We want you to come home—and we want you to be safe at home, and not keep running. Can you do that? Can you come home and be safe and go to school?"

I didn't know what to say. He was offering me a chance to come home, and I was dying to say yes. But I knew from talking to Annie and some of the other girls that a lot of girls had bounced in and out of two or even three different places—going home, getting sent back to a new program, then going home again. And I really wanted to make it work. I hated the idea of getting sent away again. But I wasn't totally sure that I could keep myself under control. I knew that the black pissing dog days had not completely gone away—and I didn't want to pretend that they had and then have it all come crashing down on me and my parents when I flamed out again.

But then I thought about the debate and helping Amanda with her mom and backing Kendra down. I couldn't have done any of that a year ago. So maybe I had gotten better, and stronger.

"I think I can," I said, slowly. "I really want to try. I've learned some things here that will help, and I know I can make a better effort. I'm stronger, I think." I tried to smile at him. "And I think my brakes are better, too, Dad."

"That's what we need to hear, Lexie. We know you've made some real progress, and Annie feels you have, too. We don't expect you to be perfect, and we know you have to keep working at handling the depression when it hits you. We want to help you do that, and not have you pushing us away, Lexie."

"I won't."

And I think I really meant it this time.

44

Annie

Instead of an over-muscled goon, this time the new owners sent a suit. Two suits, actually, one male and one female. The woman was more corporate than the man, if possible, wearing a pin-striped pantsuit and high heels. She had her highlighted hair up and carried a fancy briefcase. The man was tall, looked about forty or so, and never smiled. She introduced herself as Millicent Rosine and he said his name was Trent Ballinger.

Annie had answered the front door at Prospect, and Rosine asked to see Suzanne. While they were waiting for Suzanne to arrive from the administration building, Annie decided what the hell, I'm going to just wade in here.

"May I ask what you're here about?"

"We have an appointment with Suzanne," said Rosine, looking at the pictures in the hallway instead of at Annie.

"Is it about one of the girls, or the program . . . ?"

Rosine looked at Annie as if she was an annoying waitress and said "We'd prefer to discuss it with Suzanne."

"That's fine. Suzanne asked me to sit in because I'm the senior staff person here and know all the girls through therapy I do with them." She paused, and pushed ahead. "I assume you're from Blackoceans."

Ballinger spoke for the first time. "That's our parent company, but we work for Youth Visions."

"Does Youth Visions operate other residential programs?"

"We're in the process of acquiring several other facilities. Do you have any idea how long Suzanne will be?"

Then Suzanne walked in and apologized for being late. We all sat down in the front room.

"How can I help you?" Suzanne asked. Her tone was formal, and Annie suspected that Suzanne had known what the meeting was about.

Rosine said, "We need a record of all residents who have access to your computers. Someone has been accessing our corporate records and we've traced it back to this house."

Suzanne smiled and said "I'd be surprised if one of our girls did it; they have very limited access to our computers. What was the problem?"

"Whoever did it was trying to go through records they have no right to review." Annie could tell that the corporate team was reluctant to explain what had been accessed, and that they were embarrassed at what might have been discovered. She decided to press harder.

"Was it about corporate finances or something like that?"

Rosine focused on Annie for the first time. "Yes. Do you know anything about it?"

"I haven't accessed anything like that," Annie answered, aware that they could hear her ducking the question.

Suzanne smiled and held up her hands. "Look, let's wrap up the sparring. You already have a list of our girls because you're from the central office. Now, if you want to know who's been on the computers, it's all ten of them at some point in the past month and all of the staff—both Annie and me included." Then she asked the question Annie had just asked. "What did they get that is bothering you so much?"

Rosine was very angry by now, and said, "This girl—whoever she was—was looking at our corporate records. You apparently have no control over these girls. You should know that we are considering making major changes in—"

Suzanne had leaned forward and jabbed her finger at them. "Hold on. If you think that you can come in here and threaten us and one of our girls, you don't understand what we're doing here. These girls have been subjected to every kind of harassment you can imagine. If you want to get rid of us, fine. But if you're going to do anything to harm one of these girls, you can be assured that your names and your corporation's will be very prominent in media accounts of what's going on here." Suzanne was clearly remembering the conversation with the parents about the GAO reports and the congressional hearings, and knew this was a sore point with Blackoceans. She leaned back in the chair and smiled. "I should thank you, actually. You're helping me decide what I want to do next, and I appreciate it."

Annie wanted to jump up and cheer, but managed to restrain herself.

Ballinger said, in a calm but menacing tone, "Let's don't start making threats. We aren't going to harm anyone. We are just asking for basic information on who has been accessing our corporate records from here. That's not something that anyone should be doing with the computers that are installed here for instructional purposes."

Suzanne went back to her icy smile. "I would agree, but I would ask if you're saying that one of our students has penetrated your corporate security to get information that's not on the public record?"

Ballinger responded, "Apparently you have some students here who are rather sophisticated. We had to hire an outside expert to find out where the probe had come from, and he was able to trace it to this house. As we looked at the background of your girls, there is only one who—"

Suzanne interrupted him. "You're investigating our girls? Are you aware of the state and federal laws protecting their privacy?"

Rosine broke in. "We're doing anything we need to so that we can find out why your residents have been violating your procedures. None of these girls should be accessing the internet without your approval—and that is clearly what is happening here."

"We'll look into it. But I hope you're not violating these girls' privacy rights in ways that could create a corporate liability for you. Will there be anything else?" She was daring them to take her on directly, and Annie thought what the hell, my turn.

Annie said, "Can I tell you about my roommate from college? She's the beat reporter for the *Southern California Register* who covers children and family issues, and she's done some prize-winning work on kids' issues." She stopped and looked straight at Rosine, and then Ballinger. "Don't threaten us or these girls."

Ballinger looked back at her, and then stood up. "We're not getting anywhere, I'm afraid. You've both made your position clear. And then he looked at Annie "Don't do anything you would regret."

After they left, Annie sat back in her chair and said "Whew! This getting heavy, isn't it?"

Suzanne answered, "Yes, it is." She sighed. "I'm going to have to talk to the rest of the old leadership at the central office. If any of them are left by now." She paused and looked at Annie. "Are you sure you want to go all the way on this? They can fire both of us, just like that," she said, snapping her fingers.

"I know. But there's no way I could work here if they make the staffing and other changes they've said they're going to make. So I'm not staying. If I stayed, they'd still fire me sooner or later for something where I'd have to choose between the girls and their corporate BS. I'm ready. This isn't going to get better with BO in charge. And I need to do something I believe in."

Suzanne was quiet for a few moments, and then smiled at Annie. "Annie, I know you and the rest of the staff think I'm mostly a tight-ass." She laughed. "Actually I'm not such a bad person. I had to be tough and curt sometimes to do this job, to handle the pressure coming from the houses and from the central office. But I got into this work twenty years ago because I believed in it. Like you," she motioned at Annie, "I had a family member who had to go into the system. Only the system destroyed him. My older brother went to one of the Texas programs that the GAO investigated. He was put in isolation for twenty days and something happened. They strong-armed him, we think, and he basically cracked—his brain was harmed and he's been in and out of institutions for the last fifteen years. So I wanted to try to make at least one set of programs better. But you're right—that isn't what these bastards from BO are all about."

She paused and then said, "So let's try to figure out where we go from here."

Annie liked the "new" Suzanne—and then she realized that the person she liked had been there all the time.

As they talked, Suzanne filled in more of the Blackoceans picture for Annie. Apparently Blackoceans had made contact with a downstate legislator who was famous for his severe budget-cutting proposals. At one point he had suggested that the state prisons should force inmates to work in coal and uranium mines in the northeastern section of the state, as a way of reducing the costs of the prison system.

Blackoceans officials had made a case that their experience in running prisons, both overseas and in the U.S., prepared them to take over many of the residential facilities for youths in the state. The legislator had loved the idea, and had gone public with it, without mentioning his talks with Blackoceans. He made a speech to a statewide convention of social workers, saying that he had several friends who were taking care of their disabled children at home and that the kids in group homes and residential programs "should either be at home with their parents or locked up in prisons run by companies able to teach them about the virtues of hard work." He also claimed that the residential programs could be run at a profit once the ownership was transferred from "do-good agencies" to corporations "that know how to pinch pennies and make sure that social programs work for the taxpayers and not the inmates."

The social workers went crazy, booing him loudly, which was exactly the reaction the legislator had wanted his hard-right backers around the state to see as he prepared to run for Governor. He knew that being booed by a group of social workers would get him wide visibility, while showing him standing up to people whom his core supporters saw as being on the public dole themselves.

When Suzanne had finished bringing Annie up to date, Annie sat back and said "We are really going up against some heavyweights here, aren't we?"

Suzanne smiled and said, "Yes, but I think we can show them what some of these 100-pound girls can do when they make their minds up. And what we can do for them."

Email
From: Annie Salinas to Beatrice Salinas and Geraldine Salinas
Subject: Get out an extra pillow

Well, hermanas, looks like I'll be seeing more of you soon. That company Blackoceans that I told you about is going ahead with some really crummy changes in the program, and it's gotten to the point where I just have to leave. I'm going to miss these girls something fierce, but the way these new guys are messing up the program, if I stayed I'd just end up in a fight or spend all my time whistleblowing. Either way I'd get fired sooner or later.

Five years is a long time, and it hurts to know how much I'll leave behind. There's an intern I've been working with who really gets it, and I feel good knowing that I got her off to a good start. Wherever she goes, she'll have had a good first job where she learned a lot.

And now I'm in the job market. There are hundreds of residential programs out there, but this whole experience has soured me on working for somebody else who doesn't get it. What I'd really like to do is to start my own program and run it right from the start.

Know any millionaires? Got any good lottery tickets?

Love you,
Annie

45

Lexie

After my dad's visit, my parents and I had agreed I was going to stay for four more weeks and then come home in time for Christmas. It had gone by slowly, but I had finally gotten to the final weeks, and was dying to go home.

But as my time to leave Prospect grew closer, I found myself thinking back over the eight months and all that had happened. I remembered the feeling I had when I was talking to my dad about coming home—telling him that I had gotten stronger. I had—I knew I really had.

As slowly as the time had gone in the boring parts, I began to see the whole thing at The Houses as part of a time I knew I'd never forget—the good and the bad. Getting to know the girls, battles with the staff, trying to get closer to Sophia, seeing how Dad's work helped us understand what Blackoceans was doing, the debate and the talk with Diane Dozier about my future—all of it started to add up in a way I couldn't see when I was inside the experience. I had grown in lots of ways, more confident of myself and able to get along better with a lot of different kinds of people.

I knew I was going to miss Annie a lot. She had helped me do the work I needed to do to handle the black dog days and my worst impulses. She knew when to push me and when to prop me up. I trusted her to tell me what she really thought instead of just repeating some tired old therapy slogans and ask me what I was feeling.

And I had begun to see how much I was able to help some of the other girls. Annie had told Sophia to talk to me, and I tried to help her, though in the end it didn't work. I knew I had helped Amanda be strong with her birth mother. And we all helped Monica up in the snow when Kendra went after her. Even Laila had seemed to be able to lean on me a little when Dot Beecher brought up all that awful stuff that had so many bad memories for Laila.

Maybe Dot Beecher was right. Maybe you get better—sometimes—when you stop worrying about getting better yourself and start thinking about other people who need help.

Maybe I was stuck in a loop: they say I'm sick so I need to be cured, so I'll wait for that to happen with the meds and the therapy and all the rules here in the middle of nowhere. But maybe it doesn't work that way. Maybe I get somewhere if I worry about someone else.

The AA people talk about a "higher power." But maybe there's also a "higher need" than your own. The way it worked for me, when I stopped obsessing about what I needed—I ended up with more control over my life because I had to think about somebody else for a change.

I still had black dog days, but I had learned to see them coming and how to take the edge off them by finding something I liked to do that could keep me from falling into the "pity party" trap. I knew my parents weren't the total demons I used to make them out to be, and I knew that they had been trying to keep me from hurting myself or somebody else.

And running always works—to keep me from running.

My brakes really were stronger—having all these stupid rules bugged me a lot, but the rules make you stop and think. You know at a place like this that you can't just do whatever you want "in the moment," as a friend of mine used to say. You had to think about the next moment, and the moments after that, and the rest of your life. And you had to think about the other girls, and who you might hurt if you just kept doing whatever you wanted to, acting on impulses in selfish moments.

I knew I'd miss Annie, some of the girls, and the good times. I was going to miss the fun we had getting around the stupid rules of the program. And I knew I'd never miss the food, some of the girls, and most of the staff. I was leaving a place that felt like it was nowhere, going home to somewhere I wanted to be.

The night before I left, instead of one goodbye scene, which couldn't have happened anyway because my dad was picking me up while they were all in class, the girls came up to me separately and said their goodbyes. And I teared up each time somebody came. Most of them were leaving in the next few weeks themselves, so everyone was saying goodbye to everyone else, it seemed.

Belinda almost broke my back with a big hug and said "Stay tough, Lexie. Don't let the bastards get you down." She grinned and added, "Nobody throws me my own guns and tells me to ride out of town. Nobody."

Sheila came and winked at me and said, "I'll be in touch." I was glad that they had never caught her, and wondered what kind of a life Sheila was going to have as a super-hacker.

Laurie said "See you at Ontario Mills, girl."

Monica came by and gave me a book on law that she had gotten from somewhere. She said, "Lexie, you gave me one of the best days of my life up there—both the skiing and the Kendra backdown. Thanks so much."

Amanda was sobbing, and said "Roomie, how am I going to make it without you? I'm supposed to see my birth mom in three months—can I call you to go with me?" I told her sure. And then I told her, "Mandy, don't let her push you into anything that isn't right for you. You aren't Tammy—you are Amanda, and you are terrific."

And Laila came and gave me a haiku.

> *Lexie's going home*
> *But while she was here with us*
> *She brought some home here.*

That night after dinner we started telling stories, and it reminded me of the time after I had first gotten to The Houses when they were all telling stories and I had felt so left out.

"Remember when Laurie stuffed all the carrots from dinner in her purse?"

"Remember when that movie star came and wouldn't shake hands with any of us because she must have thought we all had social diseases?"

"Remember that girl who was only here for a few weeks who had such bad digestive problems? The Queen of Beans. We'd sit down to dinner and someone would be saying grace and you'd hear this huge ripping sound and you couldn't laugh or you'd get negatives. That girl could fart the roof off this place!"

"Remember when that new girl from Rose House ran away and got stuck in a field behind a barbed wire fence with a bunch of cows sniffing at her? She screamed so loud people from a mile away came and rescued her."

"And when somebody's mom sent her some special maple syrup from Vermont and they sent it to central office to have a chemical analysis done because they thought it was LSD?"

And then some quieter memories:

"What I liked best was nighttime when staff was downstairs, and we could talk quietly to each other without them hearing and judging us with negatives and all that BS. Just talking like normal girls on a normal sleepover. No peer reporting crap, just being normal, y'know?"

"What I liked best was when we cooked our own breakfast, and Monica got so good at French toast everyone came down to breakfast early just to make sure they got their fair share."

"Her cooking was so bomb."

"I liked it when we could go for ice cream before the ice cream place closed." The closing of the ice cream place had been like a death in the family to the girls, and our memories of it had become huge—like it was the greatest ice cream in the universe.

And at the end, we turned on the great Jack Johnson CD that one of the girls had brought from home, with a song that all of us liked to sing together, a song that said something to all of us.

> *Where'd all the good people go?*
> *I've been changing channels*
> *I don't see them on the TV shows*
> *Where'd all the good people go? . . .*

46

Annie

It was one of the saddest things Annie had ever seen outside her own family. All those girls softly singing "where'd all the good people go?" It was all some of them needed—a few good people at the right time in their lives.

Annie knew she would have to talk with Lorraine, who would make her own choice about going or staying. She hoped Lorraine would stay, at least until her internship was finished. It would be good to be able to find out how the girls were doing.

And it would be good to be home for a while, for longer than her quick trips back and forth. Annie had heard from Irene once since the family dinner, but her sisters had been tracking her more often and kept Annie posted. Irene had stayed in an apartment with her friends, was going to AA meetings, and had a sponsor who had set up some computer courses for her at the local community college. There had been one bad scene with their parents when her father had brought up all the money that had been spent on Irene's various doctors and rehab and hospitalizations. He had only mentioned it in passing, but Irene became furious and walked out of the house cursing at her father.

Bea and Gerry had taken Irene to dinner and talked her into coming back to the house, making sure that their father would not bring up Irene's financial impact on the family. They had another mostly peaceful dinner, and afterward, Irene even began calling her mother once or twice a week to tell her how she was doing. It was, as always, one day at a time, but Bea and Gerry told Annie that the days were mostly good ones so far.

As she packed up her office, Annie felt a lot of regrets. She knew she'd find another program somewhere with a few good people. She knew she'd come out all right. But she felt sad about what The Houses could have been, and she felt even sadder about all the programs that didn't even try.

And so she picked up her copy of the national directory of residential programs, and she began to flip through it, looking for a good place with some good people, somewhere worth working, somewhere girls were getting better.

Part Three

47

Annie

DECEMBER

Annie had been looking for work for two weeks and had had a few interviews, but she hadn't found anything she liked much. Her savings were adequate, and finding a job was not yet urgent. Her parents had been very welcoming as she stayed with them in her old room. But she was beginning to worry about finding something she really wanted to do.

She was taking a break at her local coffee place when her cellphone rang. It was Suzanne, who came immediately to the point.

"Annie, there are five of us who have formed a kind of underground team to oppose the takeover. We want you to come back and join us."

Annie was floored. "To oppose the takeover? How? Who's on the team?"

"Me, Diane Dozier, Deborah Wong, and Lorraine."

"Good group. But that's only four."

"Well, there's a friend of yours here who wants to talk to you."

Annie heard the phone extension pick up and then she heard, "Hey, Annie. Sure would like to have you back here."

"Greg! I thought you got promoted and decided to play it safe."

"Long story, Annie. Come back and I'll tell you about it."

Annie was silent for a few moments. Then she said, "I'll be there in the morning. This I've got to see."

She arrived at The Houses in her rental car. It had been a month since she left, and it was winter, with a light dusting of snow on the ground. The hills were completely covered with snow.

Suzanne and the other four were waiting for her in the conference room. As she walked in, she saw furtive looks in her direction from other staff in the hallway.

Annie's first question after they sat down was an obvious one. "Why haven't they fired all of you?"

"We're not sure." She smiled. "It may be that the threats you and I made to go public in our meeting with Ballinger and Rosine had an effect. We know this—they are very skittish about publicity. They were burned by congressional hearings in 2007 on their work in Iraq, and they don't want any more publicity."

Diane spoke up. "Annie, you remember that I was a Presidential intern in D.C.? I used a few of my contacts to get a sense of whether congressional staff still have these guys on their radar. It's better than we'd hoped. There will be hearings early next year on residential treatment to follow up the GAO reports of 2008 and 2009. And the staff people I've talked with said they'd be glad to invite Blackoceans to testify—and invite us at the same time! That would shine exactly the kind of spotlight on the takeover that they don't want. It would put the staff ratio changes out in view, the cuts in training and wages, the lobbying here in the state legislature, and anything else we want to call them on. If these guys were a normal corporation with a track record in residential programs, they might be able to get by. But they're already in the spotlight because of their defense contracts overseas, and they're clearly skittish about any more public pressure that makes them look bad. And they're going to lose their political support if this breaks out into congressional hearings."

"Wow. You guys have been busy." She looked at Greg. "And some of you have had a change of heart."

Greg nodded. "It's a long story, as I said on the phone, and I'd like to explain it to you when we get some time . . . together," he added hopefully. "I saw more and more of where these corporate guys are going—and I thought a lot about what you said before you left. And then I called Suzanne."

Annie knew she'd need to meet with Greg separately and see what had really happened, and if they was any chance of them getting back together. She put that little flare of rekindling aside for the moment. "What about the rest of the staff here?"

Suzanne said, "They're very nervous about their jobs, and they're mostly waiting to see what happens. Ballinger has some new people who've been spending a lot of time out here from central. They hired a former RTC director from Texas who is a lot smoother than Rosine or Ballinger were. And she's been talking to staff. So most of them are on the fence. They don't like what they're hearing about BO—" she laughed, "that's what we call Blackoceans—but the staff is playing it safe for now."

Diane said, "A few of the teachers and house staff have come up to me quietly and told me they hope we succeed, but they don't want their names used yet."

Greg said, "As soon as they saw that I was meeting with Suzanne and the rest of them, they cut me off from all corporate communications. They've been meeting a lot behind closed doors at central, and we think they'll decide what to do with us fairly soon. So we've been talking about moving first and asking for a meeting with them."

"So why call me? You guys have gotten off to a great start. What do I add?"

Suzanne said, "Let me be blunt, Annie. In addition to being a great staff member with lots of experience, you know where your values are, you're Latina, and you're good-looking. All those things matter. And we thought you could help us decide which of the girls and which of the parents might testify when we go to the congressional committee."

Annie was trying to sort out which of her attributes she was glad they noticed and which she was bothered by. But then she realized it was all a package and she didn't have the luxury of deciding which part of her background to emphasize and which to suppress. "OK. Got it. I'm in. So when are you going to meet with them?"

Suzanne said, "We wanted to see if you were aboard. We'd like to schedule it for later this week."

It was Monday, and Annie began mentally scheduling her meeting with Greg and her calls to some of the girls who had gone home recently. Right away she thought of Lexie. She looked at Diane and said, "What do you think about Lexie Crockett?"

Diane tapped the files in front of her and said, "First one on my list. That debate project she did was terrific—she'd be a great witness. And we'd like you to talk with her first."

Annie and Greg had agreed to meet at a local restaurant, and as Annie walked in she was glad to see they were there early, before the dinner crowds. Greg was seated at a table for two, watching for her. She came over to the table and sat down.

After they ordered, Annie said, as lightly as she could, "So tell me why you changed your mind."

Greg began, looking straight at her. "My dad had a simple philosophy: to get along, go along. He was a mid-level guy in a department store where I grew up in St Louis, and he wanted to make vice-president all his life. But he never made it. And I guess that and other stuff made my mom an alcoholic. She drank all day long, and hung around art galleries, and she wasn't much of a mom to me and my sister. So I got out of the house as soon as I could. She died when I was in college."

"Get along, go along."

"Yeah. But all I've been thinking about for the last few weeks is you telling me I was gutless and immature and then walking out. I replayed that conversation over and over, Annie. It really pissed me off. But I couldn't get past how strong you were, and how certain you were that you were doing the right thing. And then," he smiled, tentatively, "then I had to decide whether you were right—or just stubborn."

Annie gave him a little slack. "Could be both."

"Yeah. Could well be." He looked at her, quiet, for what seemed like a long time. Annie waited.

"I guess I always wanted my dad to stand up for something—at work, and with my mom. I wanted him to try harder to get her to stop drinking. And I envied you, Annie. Somebody taught you how to stand up. And I wanted to be like you." He paused. "And maybe change your mind about me while I was changing myself. So I called Suzanne, and here we are."

"Right. Here we are." Annie watched him, wondering if he really had the stuff to fight into the late rounds, and how much he would end up leaning on her, and how far they could go. And then she remembered his apartment, and the wonderful Orozco print of the family that he was so proud of.

And she reached across the table and caressed his face again, as she had when she walked out, and said, "Greg, I'd like to get back on the merry-go-round—if you would."

And as he stood up and came around the table to embrace her, he murmured, "More than anything, Annie."

48

Lexie

I had been home for a month, and things with my parents were going pretty well. I was going to school for a half-day, doing some online courses and having a tutor come to our home three days a week. My parents were still a little over-protective, wanting to know exactly where I was going and who I would be with. The house had been alarmed, and they had given me a cellphone with a built-in GPS so they always knew where I was. I was bummed by all the security, but as my dad said, if I hadn't run fifteen times in six months, they wouldn't need any of this. Stay put, he told me, and the security fences will come down.

And I kept remembering the last session I had with Annie the day before I left. We were in her office and she had a tear or two as she hugged me. Then she sat me down and said, "Lexie, one last piece of advice. It's partly the choices you make about who you hang out with when you get back. It's partly whether you remember any of the calm-down stuff you learned here. And it's partly whether you remember what Diane said when she talked about your future." She took my hands and squeezed them and said, "Think about your future, Lexie, not just what feels good right now in the moment. You have so much to give to people—and so much you can do to make a great life for yourself."

I met some new people, and hung out with some of my old friends—the ones that hadn't gotten me in trouble. But once I started hearing some of the rumors going around about me, I almost wished

I had changed schools. A lot of kids I had known had heard that I had been sent away, and the rumors were really bizarre. I had gotten knocked up and went away to have a baby. Or I was busted on drug charges and was in prison. Or I had run away with a guy and we traveled all over the country. Or I had flipped out and was chained to a bed in a mental hospital for ten months.

I stopped trying to deal with all the rumors and just said I went to school in another state for a while to get a break from living with my parents. Nearly everybody understood that.

I was a second-semester junior, so getting ready for a "normal" senior year was a big deal. I knew I wanted to stay home and now, running away seemed like a pretty stupid thing to do. I had found some running partners, girls who ran cross-country, and we ran every other day. My job was going to school, and handling the black dog days, and being decent to my family and friends. I knew I could do that. I was somewhere I wanted to be, and I knew what it felt like to be nowhere.

And then I met a boy. At first I worried that Joshua liked me because of all the crazy stories going around about where I had been, and I wondered if he was just looking for a freak show. But after I got to know him—we went out for lots of ice cream and talked for a long time sitting out in front of the local ice cream store—he told me that he had a cousin he was really close to who had gone to rehab twice and hadn't made it. He ended up in prison for dealing. And Joshua had watched all this happen, and had tried on his own to figure out what had happened to his cousin.

And he was funny. I never thought having a guy who could make me laugh so much would be a big deal. He was cute, with short black hair and deep green eyes. But he was funnier than he was cute. He could do weird voices, and make fun of himself, and tease me, gently at first, seeing where I was still tender. And it felt so good to have almost no pressure, just getting to know him, and talking carefully about some of my black dog stuff, seeing if he could understand it at all. He seemed to be trying, and that was what counted for now.

Then Annie called. She had called twice after I had gotten back home, just to check in. We were going to try to get together because she was in Santa Ana and I was right next door in Orange, but we hadn't done it yet.

"Hey, Lexie, how you doing?"

"I'm good, Annie, how are you?"

"Not bad." Then her voice got more serious. "We need to get together. I have something I want to talk to you about."

So we made arrangements to meet in a coffee shop off the Plaza in Orange.

"You want me to what? Testify in Congress?! No way—I'd be so nervous, I'd pee my pants."

Annie smiled. "It's not the whole Congress, silly, it's just a committee. Only two or three representatives show up, it's not that scary. Diane knows all about it and can help you get ready." She patted my hand. "It would make a great senior year independent study project."

Annie had told me about the fight that was building up between her group and the new takeover people. She had flown back to California to get some of her files and some clothes, and to talk to me.

At first, I felt all that was behind me and there was no reason to get involved. I was done with all that. But as she talked, I thought about all the girls who were left back in The Houses—and the others who would be coming along. And I finally decided I needed to do whatever I could to help out. But going to Congress to testify seemed way out of my league.

Annie disagreed. "Lexie, remember how well you did at the debate? And what Diane said to you afterward? We've talked about you, and we think you would be great. No one can express what the program is like as well as someone who has been inside it."

"I'll think about it. And I'll talk to my parents. I'm glad you're going after those guys, Annie. They shouldn't be able to just come in and wreck everything. You know there's a lot I didn't like about the program, but they could make it a lot worse."

Annie leaned forward, very serious. "Lexie, remember the group session we had when you guys were all throwing out ideas on how to change the program? What if some of those ideas were tried? What if BO leaves, and we got somebody new who wanted to try those kinds of ideas?"

"Wow. You think that's possible?"

"It's a long shot. But first we have to shine the spotlight on BO and see what they're going to do. So will you help?"

"I'll have to ask my mom and dad. Mom will probably like it, because of all her political work."

Annie's eyebrows went up. "What kind of political work?"

"Oh, she does some fundraising for the Southern California political people, I don't know which ones. She's always going to meetings up in LA. There's a guy up there she meets with a lot. Short guy with a mustache, funny name. He's in Congress. I met him once."

"Waxman? Henry Waxman?" Annie was incredulous.

"Yeah, that's the one. Why?"

"Lexie, Diane told us he was the one who held the hearings on Blackoceans a few years ago. He's great! He may be the one member of Congress they're most frightened of. Lexie, your mom may be able to help us almost as much as you could!"

When I got home I told my mom about it, and then we talked to my dad after he got home that night. At first my dad was cautious about our getting involved. He said "Lexie, going up against a big company like that is very serious business. They have many different tactics they can use to stop people from getting in their way." He was quiet for a minute. "They could even come after my business. A company that big could get to some of my customers." He laughed, but not a funny laugh. "Although if they tried, it would piss me off so much I'd probably want you to go for it." He looked at me and winked. "Maybe it's time to drive that hearse up that hill, eh?"

My mom was totally enthusiastic, and wanted to call Mr. Waxman right away. We agreed we would hold off until we knew more about what was happening. But it looked like they would let me do it. So I needed to get my head around making the trip and doing the testimony. Then I got an idea.

"Mom, I'd need new clothes to testify in Congress."

She laughed and said "Both of us would, right, Ted?"

Dad said "Of course. I can't send you to Capitol Hill looking frumpy or underdressed."

49

Annie

The group of five, as they called themselves, had scheduled a meeting with the new Blackoceans representative, whose name was Audrey Cutter. She had been appointed Senior Advisor to The Houses, but it was clear that Suzanne was now reporting to her and that she was now in charge of The Houses.

Annie and Diane had done some online background work on Ms. Cutter. She had run two programs in Texas, and both had many negative reports from former residents. The group knew that sometimes these online reports were just revenge-driven efforts by girls or parents who had experienced problems, and not always a good indicator that a program was flawed. But one of the programs had been the site of an incident reported in the 2007 GAO report.

The meeting was held in the conference room in the classroom building, and Ms. Cutter was at the head of the table when the group arrived.

Cutter began with a smile. "I appreciate all of you meeting with me. I know you have some concerns, and I want to answer any questions you have." Then she looked at Suzanne, waiting for her to speak.

"Ms. Cutter," Suzanne began.

"Please—call me Audrey."

"All right. Audrey. As you know, I've already been briefed on some of the changes the new owners are considering, and I've shared these with our group. The staffing changes, the legislative efforts you've made to change the allowable staffing ratios, the training changes, and what we've heard about the use of restraints in the other programs you're associated with—all these concern us. We'd like to know if any of these are negotiable based on our experience here with the program over several years. We believe we know a lot about these girls and what they need. And we want to make sure that our experience is still relevant to what your company is proposing to change."

Cutter smiled and replied, "As I've said, we're aware you're concerned. At the same time, we've been meeting with the rest of the staff, and it does not seem as though they all see the changes the same way you might. So for now let's just assume that the five of you are a minority of the staff—with important roles in the program, to be sure."

Annie was getting a sense of Cutter, and she could see why she had been chosen to have these conversations. She was very smooth and did not seem as likely to get rattled as the other Blackoceans staff. Her move to define the group of five as a minority was skillful, and Suzanne saw the need to counter that impression.

Suzanne said, "Well, we've also been talking to staff, and we're certain that our views express what many of them believe but are reluctant to step forward and say because they're afraid for their jobs."

"Suzanne, you know that not a single person here has been terminated. Annie," she nodded at Annie, "decided to leave on her own, and of course that was her right. But none of the rest of you have been threatened, and you won't be. We want a smooth transition that takes advantage of your skills and experience."

Greg spoke up. "We haven't been threatened, but we've had all our responsibilities wiped out—which is a pretty clear message."

Audrey responded in an even tone. "Greg, your promotion was a clear message as well. We believe you have a lot to offer the agency, and we want to be able to utilize your skills. We are still trying to determine how those might best be channeled."

She folded her hands and looked at the rest of the group. "Now, let's talk about the changes we've proposed. The staffing pattern is one which has been used in many other programs with success. We think the recruitment and training efforts that would go along with the new staffing pattern will assure all of us that we have well-trained, motivated staff in The Houses, along with the house parents in residence."

Annie spoke up. "What about restraints and isolation?"

Audrey said, "Your program has used isolation for years as a disciplinary method to help girls get control of themselves. We see the use of restraints only in extreme cases."

Diane asked "Will you meet on a regular basis with our staff to review those cases, along with the uses of discipline and other program issues?"

"Of course we will have regular staff meetings, as you have done in the past. The appropriate representatives of the house staff, the therapeutic staff, and the classroom teachers will all be included."

Suzanne then pressed harder. "Will you allow that staff group to review your budgets to see if adequate staffing, staff development, and nutritional expenses are included in the budget?"

For the first time, Audrey frowned. "No. We are a private corporation and the finances are reviewed regularly by the board of directors."

"Will you add anyone from staff to the board?"

"We would take that under advisement." Back to smiling now.

Suzanne tapped the table lightly. "Audrey, you're staying very general with your commitments, and we can hear what you're not saying. You need to know some things. We have been in touch with congressional staff who were involved in the hearings on GAO's study of residential programs. We have also talked with Congressman Waxman's staff as well as the Republicans on the committee about the shift of Blackoceans' interests from foreign operations to domestic programs, and there is some interest from that committee in holding hearings as well."

She paused for a moment, because Audrey's façade had finally dropped. She was glaring at Suzanne with such anger that Annie was afraid for a moment that Suzanne was in real danger.

Audrey exploded. "Are you threatening me?"

Suzanne was as calm as Annie had ever seen her, doing her control thing perfectly. "No, we're not. We think hearings on problems with residential treatment would be a good idea. Don't you?"

Audrey stood up. "This meeting is over, if you're coming in here and threatening us with congressional hearings."

Suzanne remained seated. "Audrey—one more thing. If there is any retribution aimed at any of us or any other staff, I know you realize it will provide that much more evidence that you have something to hide. And your financial records and profit projections are likely to become a part of the record at that point."

"Get out of this conference room and this building. We will not give you the satisfaction of being fired. Not yet. But get out of here now."

As they walked out, Greg said to Annie, "Well, that went rather well, don't you think? I mean, she didn't hit, spit, or kick. What else could we hope for?"

Annie wasn't buying the humor. "That woman is dangerous, Greg. She will not take this lying down. Their next move could be serious as hell."

The first move the Blackoceans leadership made was to place all four of the remaining staff members on involuntary paid leave. Then they waited to see if the congressional hearings were real. The Democrats and Republicans had to both agree to hold the hearings, and negotiations between the two parties' representatives were ongoing. Diane Dozier had heard from a contact that the Republicans were becoming interested because of the high costs of the residential programs, while the Democrats were more concerned about the effectiveness of the RTCs. But both sets of members on the key committees wanted to learn more, and the hearings were the best way to start that process.

A month later, when the staff of both the House Education and House Energy and Commerce committees had called to inform the company that hearings were in fact being scheduled for early spring, the four staff members who were openly opposed to Blackoceans' changes were fired.

Annie and Greg had taken some time to vacation in Hawaii. As they lay on their beach towels at Hanalei on Kauai, they talked about what they wanted to do next. Watching sunrises and sunsets over the ocean, they settled into their own cycle: first they talked about their work plans, and then they talked for a while about their personal plans. Work, personal, work—the cycle went back and forth in the eternal balancing act of young and not-so-young professionals. And as they relaxed in the warm mid-Pacific sunshine, the beckoning pathways of their lives rose into view, showing them the choices and risks they'd find on the rungs of the ladders ahead of them.

50

Lexie

As we got ready for the trip to Washington, I could tell that my parents were more nervous than I was. Diane had prepared me well, and I was just going to read our statement, so I wasn't that anxious. But my parents were off the wall. The local newspaper ran an article interviewing me when the congressional committee released the names of the witnesses for the hearing. So they both got lots of calls from their friends. I know they had spent a lot of time over the last few years trying to explain where I was and what I was doing, so maybe this would balance the books a little—as my father would say.

The funniest thing was when Justine came home from college and said some of her professors and her classmates in a political science class wanted to meet me. They had read the article in the newspaper about my testifying and they were doing some kind of project on congressional investigations. Justine wasn't groveling or anything, but she was a hell of a lot nicer to me than she had been in a long time. I said sure, I'd be glad to go up to her campus in LA and meet with them when I got back.

I couldn't resist adding, "Anything to help out a sister."

The testimony was finally written. Annie and Diane and the group had used a lot of my ideas, which we had gone over several times when we met on some conference calls. I felt very important, going to my dad's office and meeting with Annie there. We called the rest of the group on a speaker phone and went over the testimony and what

Suzanne was going to say in her part. I had suggested talking about the program the way a girl in one of The Houses would experience it from the first day she got there, feeling like she was in the middle of nowhere, and they liked my ideas.

51

Annie

Annie worked with Lexie on her presentation, and found herself listening to Lexie even more carefully than she usually did at The Houses. Like many of her peers, Lexie had a verbal tic that added a "Yeah" at the end of a sentence when she didn't know how to gracefully end a conversation and was seeking, with minimal effort, some affirmation. Annie no longer heard the word in normal conversation, because it was so frequent and so meaningless, but she mentioned it to Lexie because it would be disconcerting in testimony or responding to questions.

Lexie smiled, embarrassed, bouncing a bit in her chair, and "My mom points that out all the time. So I try to work on it. Ye . . ." she caught herself, and added, "oops."

As Lexie returned to reading the testimony, Annie watched her, thinking back to the girl she had first met a year before. Lexie was more than just a year older—she had grown in many ways. Annie knew that some of it had been because of the program, and some of it was despite the program. Some of it was in Lexie all along, needing parents and therapists and some good friends to bring it out.

And then Annie thought about all the other girls that Lexie would be representing when she gave her testimony, and said a silent prayer for all of them. And for Irene.

52

March

Rayburn Building, Room 301. House Committee on Education and Labor, Subcommittee on Youth Programs

"Our next witness is Alexandra Crockett from Orange, California. Miss Crockett, please come forward to be sworn in."

Epilogue

Within a month of the Education Committee hearings, with the congressional round of hearings coming up, Blackoceans announced that it would be selling its interest in The Houses and the other residential programs it had bought. The first set of hearings had not gone well for the company, and its refusal to provide any information about the financing of its programs had turned up the spotlight that much brighter. The company apparently decided to cut its losses and announced that it was leaving the residential treatment business for good.

Lexie got a call from Annie after the news got out about The Houses being for sale. "Guess what, Lexie? Remember the session we had in Prospect when all of the girls were making suggestions about what you would do to change things if you girls were running things?"

"Sure. That was fun, with Belinda and me working with you."

"Well, we've heard that a foundation that funds youth programs is interested in buying The Houses to experiment with new ways of running residential programs. They call it youth empowerment. It sounds as if some of the ideas you girls came up with could be on the table. I've been offered a job by the foundation. How would you like to be a consultant to the foundation if they go ahead with the purchase?"

"A consultant? What would I have to do?"

"Do what all consultants do—look wise and ask hard questions. Can you do that?"

"Sure. And I would get paid?"

"Yes."

"Wow. My dad's going to freak out."

"I'll call you when the deal goes through. In the meantime, you keep studying, keep running—the right kind of running—get yourself into college, and stay out of trouble. We can't have any delinquents working for our new company."

"You got it."

THE END

Afterword

As much as she has helped me, this is not Ashley's story. Her experience helped me capture some of the realities of residential treatment, but it is not her experience that is at the center of this particular story.

She ate the Scooters, she was handed the soap packages from the little old ladies—but it is the 14,000 other girls whose stories this book tries to tell. Some of the incidents in the story are based on generous sharing by Ashley and several other girls. But none of the girls are based on real characters.

Nor is the program meant to be about any one program or agency. The geographic details are blurred so that no one facility would be in a spotlight. There are more than two hundred programs listed in the directory of the National Association of Therapeutic Schools and Programs—and those are just the ones that belong to NATSAP. I have visited a half dozen, and carefully studied dozens more. Yet too many of these stories are real, taken from hard-won experience and continuing pain.

If the impression this book leaves is that there are some very good programs and some very bad ones—fine. If it sounds like I believe both good people and bad people run these programs—correct. The good ones make a difference, but the bad ones make it worse for girls who deserve and need so much more.

This story has an ending that is more hopeful than pessimistic. But out in the real world, the reasons to be optimistic today seem less persuasive than the reasons to worry about these programs and these girls, as well as thousands of boys in similar programs. The tendency to incarcerate is still more powerful in this country than an understanding of how to treat mental illness when it is compounded by the effects of parental substance abuse.

"Where'd all the good people go?" Some of them work in these programs. Some of them are trying to parent these girls. But we need more than these few to help overcome the bad breaks, bad parenting, and bad public policy these girls have to endure. They all deserve more help than they are getting.

I need to thank some people who have been very generous in helping me understand the world of residential treatment. In particular, Peter and Kate Dickerman and Judy Gardner shared their professional experience in residential and treatment settings. Some other advance readers who will remain anonymous have given me very thoughtful feedback from the perspectives of both staff and girls "inside."

Reading *Half the Sky*, the remarkable book by Nicholas Kristof and Sheryl WuDunn, helped frame some of the ideas about a "higher need," and so did the work of our son Rick at the extraordinary Mardan School in Irvine.

Bob and Karen Gardner provided timely access to a wonderful "writer's room" at their June Lake house. Nancy Young, as always, has helped me find precious time to write as we moved through one or two other challenges in our work and family, and gave it a great read in the final stages. Larisa Owen kept me laughing and working, as she has for rich decades of our life together, and James Owen kept an eye on things for us and helped immensely with final production. Jack Callie provided some fabulous meals along the way, and Rick, the occasional rock in our family, chased a few things down for me while this book was being written. Helen Gardner's line edits proved once again that a basic British education is at least the equivalent of an MFA program in an American university.

And Ashley helped her Papatoonie with her smiles, laughter, and immense potential, by inspiring me to write this as she moved along on her own journey. She made me take out all the "old man" talk, and we had some great times reading and writing together.

December 2010   Irvine, June Lake